DEMYAN
&
ANA

A Russian Guns Novella

Bethany-Kris

Published by Bethany-Kris

www.bethanykris.com

ISBN 10: 0-9937797-9-4
ISBN 13: 978-0-9937797-9-4
eISBN 10: 0-9937797-3-2
eISBN 13: 978-0-9937797-3-2

Cover Design © Jay Aheer

Elle,
There would be no Russian Guns without you.
You put up with me, them, and this. You listen to my crazy and
always love me through it.
You help me to be relentless, so insane. And it lets me get out the
very best even when it hurts.
Thank you.
—Kris.

CONTENTS

Chapter One

Demyan

It's one thing to have a mob boss for a father. It's an entirely different thing to have Anton Avdonin for a father.

"Are you ever going to marry that girl?" Anton asked, nodding in Gia's direction.

Gia laughed with Demyan's mother. About what, he didn't know. She looked happy and carefree.

"You're twenty-five. She's twenty-six. You're almost done with school, she already is and working. Not to mention you're living together. Shit, you might as well *be* married, son. Just get it done with already."

Demyan cocked a brow over the top of his beer bottle. "Get it done with?"

"Well, what the fuck else do you want me to say? It's not like you're making any damn effort to do it on your own."

Lifting a single shoulder in response, Demyan tipped the bottle up and swallowed a mouthful of the amber colored, bitter liquid.

"You've been in love with her forever. I wish you would make it official."

Demyan rolled his eyes. "It's not any less official just because we don't have rings and a signed marriage license. We're happy like this. She's really independent. I don't know if she will ever want to get married."

"Have you even proposed?" Anton asked pointedly. "How would you know if you don't?"

"You assume I haven't."

"If you asked Ivan for his daughter's hand like a good man, I would be the first person he called after."

Goddamn it. Sometimes it sucked to have his father be such close friends with Gia's father. Between the two of

7

them, nothing flew under their mutual radars. It had been like this since Gia and Demyan were teenagers.

"You don't understand. I'm not going to ask Ivan for something Gia doesn't want yet, Papa."

Anton's brow crinkled. "Oh."

"Yeah. I'd marry her in a heartbeat. Like first thing tomorrow morning at the courthouse if she would let me."

"Why won't she?"

Demyan didn't know.

"Is it the Bratva thing again?" Anton asked.

"No, I don't think so. We don't talk about that at all."

"Nothing?"

"Nope," Demyan said simply. "It's easier this way."

"So, fact is, that could be precisely why, but you don't know because you won't ask."

Demyan hated when his father made sense. "I love her, Papa."

"I know you do."

"Exactly. And if being together like we are is what makes her happy, I don't need more. I won't push her for more, either. She doesn't like that I'm Vor, so I don't make a point of shoving it in her face. It's only a small piece of us, but not all. I'm going to keep my focus on the better parts."

"Fair enough," Anton said, but his smile didn't ring true. "And when were you planning on telling me, anyway? Or at least, your mother."

"Tell you what?"

"That Gia's pregnant."

Demyan choked on his second swig of beer. Coughing, he wouldn't meet Anton's intense gaze. It was really fucking difficult to have a father so incredibly observant. "Why would you think she's pregnant?"

"Are you denying it, then?"

Shit.

Shit. Shit. *Shit.*

Demyan didn't lie to his father. He never had.

"You always told me never to answer a question with a

question, Papa."

Deflecting was a plan. A shitty one, maybe, but one.

Anton kept looking at Demyan in that way of his that made his son's nerves grow. "She likes her red wine. Always has. She refused it three times today."

"So?" Demyan placed his beer on the side of the barbeque. "She has to work tomorrow. The last thing she needs is to be teaching twenty kindergarteners with a hangover."

"Point taken," his father agreed, smirking. "Except, she turned green at the sight of the raw meat earlier and said it smelled awful. The meat was across the damn room. Demyan, since when have you known Gia to hate meat?"

Since she found out she was pregnant eight weeks ago.

Demyan tried to stay quiet. He did. And failed like a fucker. "Please don't make me tell you just because you have to know everything about everyone or you go insane. Seriously, you should see a fucking therapist about that shit or something. Not everything is your business, Papa."

"I'm the boss. Everything is my business if I want it to be."

"This isn't *business*; it's my life."

"And I'm your father, which makes you my life."

True enough, Demyan thought. The same way Anton always knew all, the man also just seemed to know everything about his son. For the most part, Demyan was grateful to have the close-knit relationship he did with his father. It was a solid foundation for his sometimes unpredictable and fast-paced life.

"You've never had to lie or hide things from me because I've always given you the space to be open and honest without fear of judgement," Anton said softly. "Why start now?"

"I'm not hiding it, Papa."

"Is there a reason why you two are keeping it quiet? It's not like your mother and I would be angry. Ivan and Eva already have three grandchildren; Gia's not a teenager and neither are you. You're both well-off, you work hard, and you're more than capable of caring for a child. What's wrong?"

"Nothing," Demyan rushed to say, irritation rising.

"Is she considering terminating—"

"Christ, *no!*" The fifteen or so guests to the afternoon barbeque turned to stare at Demyan's exclamation. He spun his back to the people and glowered at his father. "Thanks."

"You're good at drawing attention if nothing else," Anton said, tipping up his bourbon to sip. "Showing emotions is the only flaw in your character. It always was."

"I don't need the reminder."

"Somehow, you need to learn how to curb the instinct to react, Demyan. You've got everything else going for you—leadership, intelligence, charisma, and you're cunning as fuck. You can draw fear just as easily as you lull someone into a false sense of comfort. None of those things are worth shit if you can't control your surface emotions. This is the one thing I can't teach you. It has to be learned from the habit of beating back the impulse, son."

"I know," Demyan said quietly. "I'm working on it."

"Work harder. There are a lot of eyes on you in the Bratva right now. You're twenty-five-years-old and just starting to seriously dip your feet into the business. Many of them believe I should have made you forgo college because they think it useless. Time wasted there could have been better spent learning the streets. I wanted you to have choices. Don't make me regret letting you find your own way, Demyan."

Demyan nodded tightly. "I'll get a handle on it, Papa."

"Do that, and fast. If nothing else, manipulate how you want others to see you. Outbursts are perfectly fine when done correctly and used to motivate something, be it fear or whatever else. Random nonsense like that is nothing more than a sign of weakness someone will use against you. Especially if your outbursts focus on one thing—or rather, someone—in particular."

Without directly saying it, his father meant Gia. Demyan got the point.

"Do not bring unneeded and unwanted attention on those you care for because of your inability to remain calm," Anton said. "The harder the exterior, the less likely someone will be to try and make it crack."

"All right. I get it."

Anton sighed, eyeing his son from the side. "She is, yeah? Pregnant, I mean."

"Yes. Fourteen weeks yesterday. We were waiting until the first trimester passed and after that, a good time to sit everyone down. But, you and your fucking freaky perceptiveness had to go and ruin that. So again, thanks. Are you happy, now?"

Anton grinned stupidly. "Very. Huh. Vine will be pleased. Our first grandbaby."

Demyan stared at the sky, exasperated. This was how most of their conversations went. "You're ridiculous."

"Oh, I know. Your mother never fails to remind me."

"Seriously, go talk to a therapist about that shit," Demyan muttered.

"No. They wouldn't understand."

They probably wouldn't. His father was the kind of crazy even a therapist couldn't fix.

• • •

"Is the nausea gone?" Demyan asked.

Gia nodded as she settled into his lap. "Also, I think I want a hamburger. Now that the meat isn't all gross and bloody, they don't look so bad."

Demyan snorted. Pregnancy was insane. He didn't pretend to understand Gia's experience. For him, it was off the charts. Anxiousness walked alongside excitement.

He was going to be a father.

A *father*.

Holy shit. Unbelievable.

Demyan didn't know how it happened. Well, yeah, he knew why. It was more the when that he couldn't place. They weren't safe every time. Gia was the only girl who could muddle up his rationale so he didn't care about that sort of shit.

"Love you, *katyonak*."

Gia would always be his little kitten with claws.

"Love you," she echoed.

Gia's soft mouth touched down to the underside of his jaw. She squirmed in his lap. Demyan squeezed her bare thigh playfully. He didn't bother to hide the pleasure rolling through his bloodstream at her sigh.

"Stop that or I'm taking you home."

Gia grinned slyly. "Not until I get my hamburger."

"You better hurry, then. I'm hungry, too."

"Not for food."

"Oh, definitely not for food."

Gia stood from his lap, her pinky finger staying hooked with his until their hands unwittingly broke apart. Not five seconds after Gia left, Demyan's mother sat down beside him on the bench.

"Happy birthday, baby."

Demyan gave his mother a look. "Twenty-five and I'm still your baby."

"Of course, Demyan," Viviana said, smiling brightly. She patted his jean-clad knee. "You know, I always thought it would be awful to have your birthday the day after Independence Day."

"My birthday's always been good, Ma."

"I know. Anton loves to celebrate your day more than his own, I think. My worries were useless, huh?"

"They usually are where I'm concerned," Demyan joked.

"Not always. How are your classes at college going?"

Demyan tried not to frown. His mother was prickly about the topic of him finishing school. He worked hard toward his degree as a lawyer focusing on criminal defense. With his efforts in the Bratva piling up, he dropped two classes to free

12

some time. It added another year to his schooling. He also quit football two semesters earlier because he couldn't keep everything up. The last thing he wanted to do was explain that to his mother. It would only piss her off something fierce.

"Everything is great, Ma," Demyan half-lied.

Viviana raised a single brow as she stared across the pool to the other side of the yard where cabañas were set up for the guests. "Who is that man, Demyan?"

He followed his mother's gaze. The guy she noticed chatted with a good friend of Demyan's from college. Well, good was a bit of a stretch. Freddie was an associate who he worked some of his Bratva business through. The two first met on the football field.

Demyan learned quickly while attending private schools that the richer a person was, the darker their secrets. Freddie, like Demyan, was well-connected to the high-society scene, but not in the way someone would expect. Not all drug dealers looked like shady fucks on the street corner.

The guy chatting with Freddie was someone Demyan didn't know at all. He must have come along with his friend.

"I'm not sure, Ma."

Viviana's gaze narrowed. "He was talking to your sister earlier."

Demyan sighed. "Ana is twenty-one. She's going to talk to boys."

And on occasion, be the biggest, raging bitch on the planet, he added silently.

Demyan loved his sister, no doubt about it. Problem was, he and Ana were on two completely different wavelengths. Ana's focus never diverted from her competition-level swimming and love for literature. She thought Demyan was just a thug playing with guns. They never clicked as siblings, not in a close bond sort of way.

"My problem isn't her talking with men, Demyan. It's when she talks to a guy who hangs out with a man like Freddie."

So, his mother did know why Freddie sometimes chummed around with Demyan.

"Freddie is good. He's not going to bring trouble to our doorstep. He knows better than that, Ma."

"He better. And I hope, for that young man's sake, your father doesn't see him chatting with Ana like he was earlier."

Demyan's brow crinkled in his confusion. "What do you mean like he was?"

His relationship with his sister might be like skating on a patch of thin ice, but Demyan would still lay down his life for her. That's what family did. Now that he thought about it, he didn't like Ana messing around with a guy he didn't know, either.

"Nothing," Viviana said a little too quickly. "It was nothing. I should go find your father."

Viviana was gone before Demyan could press his mother for more. Gia caught his eye. She balanced two plates in the palms of her hands. He stood to take a plate from her.

"The quicker we eat, the faster we can get home to dessert."

Demyan smirked. Christ, he loved his girl. "You could take your plate with you."

Gia stood on her tip toes to kiss him. "Nope. Half the fun is waiting for your prize, Demyan. Happy birthday."

• • •

"You," Demyan barked.

Ana looked away from the guy flirting with her, surprise flitting across her face at Demyan's intrusion. Really, he wouldn't be bothered by a guy chatting his sister up, but not knowing who that guy was unsettled him. So, Demyan found Freddie and asked who the fuck his guest was.

Cavan Dolan. Trouble with a capital T and that was something the Avdonin family didn't need in any shape or form. The guy was well-connected to the Irish mob, considering his uncle was the boss and Cavan was the man's only heir.

He hailed from Detroit, apparently. All Freddie knew was Cavan had been sent to New York for some chill time. The Irish mob had a small syndicate in the state, so that was likely where he was doing his business.

"Go into the house, Ana."

Ana lifted a single brow, indignant. "Excuse me?"

"Go into the house."

Cavan Dolan "Hey, we're not—"

"You can shut up," Demyan ordered. "Go, Ana."

Something in the lilt of his tone must have worked because Ana pushed off the side of the house and disappeared around the corner. Demyan waited until he was sure she was far enough away not to hear the conversation before he rounded on the guy.

"You must have a mighty set of balls to crash my birthday," Demyan said, getting more pissed off by the second.

"Came with Freddie. We've got some business to chat and he invited me along."

"Good to know. I'll be sure to find another middleman for that sector if he's working more than mine. I'm only going to give you one chance to get off my father's property before I find him and let him know who you are. Understood?"

Cavan's gaze narrowed. "I wasn't doing anything wrong, Demyan."

"Doesn't fucking matter. We don't mix with other families. Not in business, and definitely not in play. Stay the fuck away from my family and especially my little sister. Ana isn't the kind of girl who messes around with guys like you. We don't need your brand of trouble around here. Leave."

Cavan smirked. "What if she doesn't want me to leave her alone?"

Demyan's blood boiled. "Stay away from my family, asshole."

Chapter Two

Ana

Water was a sacred place for Ana Avdonin. Crystal clear and pure, it washed away her stress and took away her thoughts. It allowed her to focus on only the water and the time clock she needed to beat.

"Ready, Ana?" her coach asked.

Ana nodded from her perch on the starting board. Saturdays were devoted to training and this one was no exception.

"Set."

Ana adjusted her stance. She bent her knees, leaned forward, and put her hands high together.

"Go!"

The shock of the cold pool barely registered when Ana cut through the water. She felt more at home in the comfort of a pool than anywhere else. She was undefeated in the long distance using the front crawl stroke technique. Ana's weakness came in her first half-lap where she lost at least five-tenths of a second.

Sure, that didn't seem like much, but it was a hell of a lot in a short race when she couldn't make it up later. Time the team couldn't afford for her to be losing this season.

Ana knew she was close to the wall and put her hand out to hit the sensors that stopped the clock. She popped up to the surface of the water, inhaling hard as she turned to look at the time.

"Still off by at least three-tenths," she heard her coach shout from the other end. "You were closer the last time."

Ana yanked her cap, goggles, and nose plug off before tossing them to the side of the pool. "Fuck!"

"Don't start that cussing nonsense. Just get your butt out

of the water and do it again. We'll figure it out."

Ana pointed at the large time clock above the other end of the pool. "Are you sure that goddamn thing is even calibrated correctly for the sensors? I swear to God I'm beating that mark at home every time!"

"Yes, Ana. It's checked weekly. There's nothing wrong with the clock."

Something was wrong with her, then. Something she didn't know how to fucking fix.

"I need a break, coach."

"We've only been at this for—"

"I need a break," she repeated more forcefully.

"Fine. Thirty minutes and then you're back on the start board. Got it?"

"Whatever."

• • •

"Tall, not so dark, but very handsome coming our way. Ana, he's looking at you."

Ana perked up at Missy's teasing. "What?"

Missy tilted her head to the side. "There."

Sure enough, Cavan was making his way to Ana and her teammates where they sat on the benches outside of the pool complex.

She wasn't entirely sure what to make of Cavan's appearance. She met him at her brother's birthday party a few weeks ago. While he was good to look at, there was a lot about him that felt like a warning for her to back off, too. Nevertheless, he kept showing up at the oddest times when Ana wasn't expecting him to. Last week he waited after her third class of the day. The week before that he texted her cell phone, but she had no idea how he got the number.

Cavan's interest in her was as clear as day. Ana had to admit she liked he was seeking her out, but the enigmatic vibe he carried around was off-putting. Some girls might love the mystery of a guy. As if it made him an unattainable being they wanted to tame or whatever, but not Ana. She wanted to know the whole deal upfront—who he was, what he was, and what the fuck he wanted. Especially when it came to her.

"Check out the bad boy," Cam, another one of Ana's teammates, said. "I bet he's a whole package of some kind of crazy fun."

A catcall followed from Missy.

Ana felt heat rise in her cheeks. "Shut up, you idiots."

"Didn't know you had it inside to catch a guy like him," Missy said, winking.

"You do know who her father is, right?"

"So, what's Anton Avdonin got to do with his daughter getting a piece of ass?" Missy asked.

Ana grinded her teeth. Her last name drew attention. She couldn't hide her father's Russian mob boss status. True, it gave her respect, but it could also put her in awkward positions. People assumed things about her. She didn't like that.

Missy reached over and slapped Cam. "Oh, have you met Demyan? He's ... yeah, like *whoa*. So intense."

"And taken," Ana added pointedly.

Cam shrugged. "For some guys, that doesn't matter."

Ana could play those games, too. "He's also got a baby on the way. Did I forget to mention it?"

"Oh," Missy said.

"Yeah. Don't go fucking around my brother. Gia wouldn't hesitate to cut you for it. I'm not even kidding."

Demyan might not be Ana's favorite person in the world, but Gia was like her older sister. It would be a cold day in hell before one of Ana's girlfriends had a chance with her brother. Better to cull that nonsense before it even began.

Ana didn't give her teammates a chance to respond before she left the bench with her water bottle in hand. She met Cavan halfway down the entrance walk. "Hey."

"Hey," Cavan said, grinning. "You didn't answer my texts this morning."

"Training," Ana explained, waving a hand at the building.

"On Saturdays, this is where I am from seven until four. My phone gets left at home. No distractions."

"Pretty serious business, huh?"

"For me it is."

Cavan leaned forward, his fingers slipping under the towel wrapped around Ana. Moving the fluffy white cotton just an inch, he raised a brow at her standard one-piece, black racing swimsuit. "No bikini to show off those assets of yours? Damn, I was hoping for a show."

Ana scoffed. "You're a pig and I have five minutes to get back on the starting board."

Cavan let the towel go. "Go out with me tonight."

"What?" Ana wasn't sure she heard him correctly.

"Me and you. Somewhere. Tonight. Sound good?"

Ana thought about it for a minute. When she first met him, Cavan was hanging around with Freddie, a guy Demyan had by his side a lot. Ana didn't know why her brother and Freddie were friends, but she knew they went to the same college. There was definitely more to it though because her father always invited Freddie into his office to *talk*.

Talking meant business.

Ana had no desire to get involved with someone doing business on the Bratva side of things. For one, because she didn't trust herself to have faith in a guy like that. And secondly, she didn't want to go messing around in her brother's business.

"How do you know my brother?" Ana asked.

Cavan waved his arms wide. "I don't."

"You were at his party."

"Freddie wanted me to come along. We were supposed to hang out together after. It's the first time I met Demyan."

"Oh," Ana said quietly.

"Yeah. So, tonight?"

"Maybe. You keep sending me messages and showing up at the oddest times, but I don't even know your last name."

"Dolan. Cavan Dolan."

Something about his last name seemed familiar, but Ana

brushed it off. "Why me?"

"I don't know. Something about you, I guess."

"Okay. Tonight. Pick me up at my apartment at eight. I have to make face and go to a dinner first."

"You're all mine after, right?"

Ana laughed lightly. "Something like that."

• • •

"You're late." Viviana uncrossed her arms and shooed at her daughter impatiently. "Hurry, hurry."

"Sorry, Ma," Ana said, kicking off her shoes. "Daddy isn't mad, right?"

"At you? Psht. Don't even try to joke. You look fine enough to have dinner like this."

"I smell like chlorine. It'll only take me ten minutes to shower."

"Like I said," Viviana drawled, pushing on her daughter's lower back as she directed her toward the dining room. "You're late and our guests are already here. Be good and I'll love you for another day. Indulge your father like I know you can. No cheap shots at your brother. Gia is just starting to show but please don't point it out or say anything unless she does first. Ready, set …" Her mother pushed her into the room full of faces she didn't recognize. "Smile, Ana."

Scratch that. She recognized some. Ivan, her father's best friend, and his wife Eva sat on one side of the table with Demyan and Gia, who didn't look particularly pleased to be sitting where she was. Anton sat at the head of the table like he always did while her mother took a seat at the other end. The faces staring at her from the other side of the table were unknown but for one.

Sofia Vasin. She came from a mafia family similar to Ana's. It gave her a good indication of just who the unfamiliar people sitting at the table were.

Oh. Shit. *Well, then.*

Ana suddenly understood why Gia seemed pissed.

Sofia was an old flame of her brother's … or something of that nature. Ana wasn't entirely sure what they had been together. *Something*, anyway.

A man sat beside Sofia who looked to be Ana's father's age. A woman sat to his side, and another young man beside her.

That man … he was gorgeous with a chiseled jaw sporting faint stubble, lips pulling into the hint of something sly and tousled blond hair framing his face. It stuck Ana in the chest as the guy regarded her with dark blue eyes. He couldn't be much older than she was.

She briefly considered Cavan's good looks with his reddish-blond curls and green eyes, but he didn't have quite the same effect on her insides like this guy did.

"Sorry, I know I'm late," Ana said, breaking eye contact with the young man.

"It's fine, sweetheart," her father said. "Koldan saved your chair."

Koldan. Definitely a Russian.

Anton nodded at the guests. "Who have you met already, Ana?"

"Sofia," Ana said as she sat down, trying to ignore the sharp blue gaze settling on her from the next seat. She offered Sofia a smile down the table. Sofia wasn't a terrible person or anything. Ana didn't hold any ill-will on her for whatever went down with Sofia and Demyan a few years ago. "Hey."

Sofia winked. "You look good. You're all grown up."

"She's getting there," Anton agreed, chuckling. "Scaring the fuck out of me every step of the way."

Ana clicked her tongue. "I don't do anything to scare you, Papa."

"Being a girl is enough," Ivan put in from his side of the table. "Trust me."

"Truth," the unknown older gentleman stated with a smile.

Anton cleared his throat, quieting the laughter around the

21

table. "Ana, this is the Vasin family from Jersey. I'm sure you know a little about them, considering Sofia …" Her father trailed off with a wince in Viviana's direction. "Anyway, this is Adrik, an old friend of mine. Cora is his wife. Beside you is Koldan, their son."

Ana said hello, refusing to meet the eyes of the man at her side again. She didn't need to feel like she was off kilter at the dinner. Her father talked about it for the last month which led her to believe it was important, for whatever reason. Likely for one she didn't want to know.

"Introductions are done. I'm starving. Can we eat, baby?" Anton asked his wife.

Viviana nodded. "Let's eat."

The food was served and quiet conversations flowed between the people at the table.

"How far along?" Cora asked Gia.

"Twenty weeks."

Adrik made a face. "I don't understand this week nonsense. Wasn't it always counted in months?"

"Divide it by four, Papa. She's five months," Koldan said.

"Thank you, but I'm aware of how many months, smartass."

"Did we finally find out the gender?" Viviana asked from the far end.

Ana couldn't help but notice how every man at the table perked at that question.

Anton rested his fork on the table. "Yes, have we? Boy or girl?"

"No," Demyan said, brushing his thumb along Gia's cheek. "The baby wouldn't cooperate yesterday. We have another one scheduled in a month."

"Any names?" Sofia asked softly.

Ana was surprised Sofia had asked the question at all.

Gia tensed across the table, but still answered. "We have a family name for a boy."

"Oh?" Anton shot a look down to his wife. "What's that?"

"Roman Ivan," Demyan said quietly.

Ana's mother made a sound she couldn't decipher. "But that's … it's not Russian."

"Actually, it can be," Koldan said. "The name Roman is derived from the Latin *Romanus*. It literally means roman. Lots of cultures use it, including Russians."

"See," Adrik said pointedly, looking at Anton. "Like I said earlier, too smart for his own good and doing fuck all with it."

"Not nothing. I'm working for you," Koldan replied, a cocky smirk twisting his lips.

Ana didn't like how his smirk made her mouth go dry, or the fact Koldan passed her another heated glance before he went back to his food. Except she did like it. Entirely too much.

"I like that name," Anton said, smiling. "Ivan?"

"Hell, my name is in there. Yes, I like it."

"What about a name for a girl?" Ana asked, curious.

Gia sighed. "We can't agree on that one."

Ana noticed Sofia's smile out of the corner of her eye. She hoped the girl wasn't being nice just for show.

"My bet is on the baby being a girl," Sofia said. "Congratulations."

• • •

"Those things will kill you," Ana said as she closed the front door.

Koldan looked over the cherry red tip of his cigarette. He exhaled a heavy cloud of smoke into the night sky. "Nothing fun comes from anything good for you."

Ana laughed. "The problem with trouble is it always starts out as fun."

"Yeah, well, I like a little trouble mixed in with my fun."

Ana learned over dinner that Koldan was a few months younger than she was. The soul in his stare made him feel older. His striking features caught in the shadows of the night, making him appear dark and sexy.

Ana forced back her odd desire as Koldan said, "You're headed out."

"Yep. I'll be going back to my apartment, so I probably won't get to see you again. It was nice to meet you, though."

Koldan flashed her a cunning smile, adding to his appeal. "Oh, I don't know. I think I might see you around again, Ana."

The cigarette was tossed to the pavement. Koldan passed by her to go back into the house. Ana was acutely aware of the heat of his tall, muscular frame. Before the front door closed, Koldan added, "Have a good night, *krasivyy*."

Ana blinked, her heart thudding hard and fast. He called her beautiful.

Chapter Three

Demyan

"You went out for coffee with her?" Gia asked, her cheeks turning pink.

Demyan blew out a heavy breath of air, frustrated. "Sofia invited me. I didn't want to be an asshole and our fathers are good friends, babe. I can't shun a fellow family like that. It was just a coffee. Nothing more."

"She's an ex—"

"She's a girl I fucked around with a couple of times when I was eighteen," Demyan corrected harshly. "We weren't anything important and we still aren't. Christ, Gia. What's with the jealousy? This isn't like you at all."

Gia's hurt was obvious, but Demyan didn't know how to fix it. He hadn't done anything wrong. Not as far as he could see.

"Exactly, Demyan. You've been with her. She knows you, okay? We're together. We're having a child in a few months. You have no reason to be hanging around with a girl you messed with for any reason. *None.*"

Demyan bit the inside of his cheek to hold his words back. He didn't want to say something he might regret or hurt his lover further. After the dinner two weeks earlier with the Vasin family, things had been tense to an extreme between him and Gia. Demyan realized she was feeling insecure over Sofia, for whatever reason, but he just couldn't understand why.

He loved Gia and only her. She had every piece of him there was to give.

"I'm sorry, Gia. I really didn't think of it in that way because it was innocent. She's going to be in the city for a couple of more weeks while she visits some friends. I'll let her know she needs to keep her distance while she's here."

Gia wrapped her arm around her middle and rubbed at her forehead with her other hand. "We weren't together when you were messing around with her back then, so how can you say you two didn't have something going on beyond the physical?"

"She didn't want to be a couple, she still lived in Jersey and I just started college," Demyan answered honestly. "And in case you have forgotten, you and I were fucking around on and off back then. I was still, just like I am today, head over heels in love with you, babe. What's really going on here? Tell me what I'm missing, Gia, please."

"She's beautiful, Demyan."

That did nothing to answer his question. "So?"

"*So?*"

"Because she's pretty I must want to fuck her?" Demyan asked, irritated. "That's ridiculous."

"No!"

Demyan jerked back from the anger in Gia's voice like she'd slapped him. "Whoa. Seriously, what am I missing here, Gia?"

"I'm sick most of the day. I'm tired even after I've slept twelve hours. I'm five and a half months pregnant and I look five and a half months pregnant. You go out for coffee with a beautiful girl, don't bother to tell me until you get home, and you can't figure out why that might make me feel bad, Demyan?"

Oh. Fucking hell. Didn't she know how goddamn gorgeous she was to him?

"Gia—"

"Don't bother," she said, sounding defeated. "I'm over it. I want to go to bed."

Ah, no. Demyan didn't think so. They weren't ending the day with frustration and pain between them like this.

Demyan crossed the small space separating them before Gia could react. He held her face in his palms, tilting her head up under his urging so he could crush his mouth down to hers. The softest squeak of surprise left her soft lips before she kissed him back. It was such a familiar dance for him—kissing her, loving her—that it ached deep in his chest. There was no one Demyan loved more than Gia. He released her face long enough to tangle his fingers into the blonde curls falling down her back.

"You are so beautiful," he whispered fiercely. "It's fucking insane what you do to me and what you do for me. Not for one second have I ever thought you weren't beautiful, especially now. I wouldn't ever, Gia. You're mine, babe. I love you. There is no one on this earth more important to me than you."

Gia released a shaky exhale, her blue eyes watering as she met his stare. "I'm sorry for being jealous."

"Don't be. I get it. It won't happen again. I promise."

"Your baby is making me crazy," she mumbled.

Demyan laughed deeply. "Yeah, but you're my crazy."

• • •

Two weeks later, Gia had Demyan in bed, promising a surprise. Her surprises were the best kind whenever it involved her and a flat surface as far as he was concerned, so he indulged her little game.

"Close your eyes."

Demyan did as he was told, placing his arms behind his head all the while.

"Ready?" Gia asked, straddling his waist in a way that had his cock growing thick.

"Yep."

"Okay … look."

Demyan opened his eyes to a black and white sonogram picture of his child's face. It wasn't the first time he saw the baby, but it was the first clear image of the child's profile. It was fucking amazing.

"Look at that," Demyan said, his grin widening by the second. He leaned up on his elbows to get a better look. "The little nose slopes just like yours."

"I know, right. She was sucking on her thumb, too. It was so cute, but they wouldn't let me take a video. I don't know why. Hospital policy or some bullshit. I think the tech was just being a bitch."

Demyan choked on air. He didn't care about hospital policies or any of that other nonsense. "*She?*"

"Yeah." Gia bit her lip; her excitement was palpable. "It's a girl, Demyan."

Demyan cursed lowly. He missed finding out the gender of his first child because of some stupid test worth twenty percent of his overall grade. Un-fucking-believable.

"Hey, don't," Gia said gently, placing the sonogram picture to the bed. Her warm hands slid under his shirt and up to his chest, making his heart and lungs stop. "I know that look, Demyan. Don't be angry. The test was important. You've been to every other appointment. There'll be more. It was only one."

"An important one, Gia," he argued. "God, a girl?"

"A girl."

"A girl," he repeated. "*My* daughter."

"Are you happy?" Gia asked, her fingers tapping a tantalizing beat to his skin. "You were pretty set on the boy name and all. I thought maybe that's what you wanted."

Demyan all but shouted his joy. "Fuck, yes. I am … *ecstatic.* We're having a girl, Gia."

"I know." Gia's face lit up. "You want to tell the world or no?"

"No," Demyan said instantly. "Not right now. Christ, come here."

With no warning, Demyan grabbed Gia by the waist and flipped them over in one movement. He fit perfectly to her body with her thighs tight around him as he rained kissed down her face and neck. Running his hands down her sides, he fisted her dress and dragged the fabric up until the pink lace of her panties were exposed and she was grinding her core against the bulge in his jeans.

As far as he was concerned, the best way to celebrate her surprise was for him to love her like only he knew how.

Gia's blissful sighs filled the room and Demyan to the brim until he was so hard it ached and he couldn't think about anything else but being buried inside of her. Demyan made quick work of ridding them both of their clothing. His fingers slid along her slit, finding her slick with the silky wetness of her arousal. She was always ready for him, her body responsive and wanting. Christ, he loved this girl like nobody knew.

Gia's nails scraped gently down his pecs as he kissed her hard and deep, wanting her closer. Two of his fingers plunged into her sex as her tongue flicked to the seam of his mouth "*God*, Demyan."

"What do you want, babe?" he asked with a huskiness building in his tone. "Soft or hard?"

"I'm not breakable," she mumbled against his lips while his fingers stroked inside her clenching walls. "Just pregnant."

"Oh, I know. Thought I should give you the option."

Demyan withdrew his fingers from Gia's body and flipped her over onto her hands and knees, sending her blonde curls flying in a mass of waves over the bed. He kissed her back, tasting the flavor of her skin with his tongue while his hands palmed her ass. Gia groaned, fisting the duvet as she backed into his groin.

Demyan's fingers found her sex again. He used his one hand to fuck her while his other wrapped around her thigh to reach between her legs and circle fast strokes to her clit. Gia cried out when Demyan didn't relent in the pace or power of his motions. It wasn't long before her tart juices were soaking his hand, her thighs shook, and she was coming hard around his digits with a shout.

He didn't wait for her to catch her breath. His fingers left her sex just long enough to be replaced by his cock. Sliding into her wet, hot channel blew away every thought in his mind. She was still bearing down from her orgasm, her walls contracting like a vise around his shaft when he bottomed out inside her.

"Shit, yeah," Demyan hissed, a white heat searing through his senses. "Christ, you feel good."

"Stop talking and *fuck me*," Gia whimpered.

Demyan held Gia up a little higher with one arm. He took her how she wanted with hard and long thrusts that sent her breathy moans spinning into high cries. Her fingernails dug into his arm around her middle and the soft curls of hair tickled his chest as she tossed her head back.

Demyan knew this woman. He understood her cues, her body and how to work it. There were many females for him during the periods of their splits when they were younger, but only Gia had been the one to teach him *her*. His first time was a messy, fumbling encounter with a girl older than him in the backseat of a car. His next had been Gia. There was never a time when he didn't regret not waiting for her back then, but everything he knew about what she liked, needed and how to fuck her—*love* her—was because of Gia.

When her fingernails scored deeper and her walls fluttered around him, Demyan pulled her back into his chest, turned her face and kissed her mouth. His teeth nipped at her bottom lip, giving her the bit of pain that would heighten the euphoria of her orgasm, as she came undone around him.

"There it is," Demyan murmured. Fuck, he was so close. "Ready, babe?"

"So ready," Gia said, breathless and giggling. "Don't hold back."

Demyan let his hold on her go. Gia caught herself with her palms down to the bed. In the next second he was pounding into her harder than before, letting the pressure build in the base of his spine until he was about to explode.

"Fuck, fuck, fuck," Demyan growled.

Demyan's vision blurred with the force of his release. A rip of pleasure tore through his insides as he emptied himself deep into Gia.

Spent, he withdrew from her body and pulled them both down to the bed, adjusting his lover so she was tucked snugly into his side and his hand was placed on her slightly rounded midsection.

Gia sighed. "I should surprise you more often."

"Yes, do that. Fuck, where's the phone?"

"Why?"

"Tell the world, you know," Demyan said before he kissed her naked shoulder.

"Can we get dressed first?"

"No, I have to call my father."

"He's not going to know if you took an extra couple of minutes—" Gia's words cut off and she snorted in the cutest way. "Never mind, yes he would. He knows everything about everyone. He's crazy like that."

"Crazy is one way to put it. Grab the phone."

Gia leaned over to grab both their cellular phones off the nightstand. She tossed his phone over before plucking up her dress and turning her home screen on.

"Eva will be pissed off something fierce if she doesn't hear it first," Demyan said, keying in his father's number. "So will Anton."

Gia agreed. "That's why I grabbed both phones. Call Anton, I'll call Ma."

"Sexy and smart. I picked a good one with you, huh?"

"No, I picked a good one," Gia said, poking his side. "Call your father."

Demyan grinned, hit the call button, and put the phone up to his ear. Gia's call to her mother was still ringing when Anton picked up Demyan's. She pulled the dress he had yanked off her earlier back on as he focused in on his call.

"*Privyet*, Demyan," his father greeted.

"Hey. Where are you right now?"

"Home. Convincing your mother to make me a pie. Why?"

"I'm not making you a damn pie, Anton, so there's no convincing going on here," Viviana said in the background. "There's a half of a fucking cheesecake in the fridge that you wanted me to make yesterday. Eat that."

31

"There's a shop down on the boardwalk that sells apple and cherry ones, Vine." Demyan laughed when his father added lower, "Twenty bucks says she's going to make me a pie, now."

"I'm not stupid enough to take that bet, Papa."

"Hey, Ma," Gia said, moving to the edge of the bed.

Demyan reached out to stroke Gia's back as he said to his father, "Put the phone on speaker."

"Why?" Anton asked. "You know I don't like doing that. Bad enough the feds listen to all my conversations as it is."

"Just fucking do it. You're ruining the moment with your craziness."

"What moment, Demyan? You can't call someone and have a *moment*."

"Put it on the goddamn speaker so Ma can hear this, Papa."

"Yeah, we found out," Gia told her mother on her call.

"Alright, it's on," Anton grumbled. "Vine, don't leave yet."

"What, why?" his mother asked.

Gia looked over her shoulder and Demyan nodded. Together, they announced the gender of the baby. "It's a girl."

Demyan wasn't sure how Gia's mother was reacting to the news, but his phone call had gone entirely silent. But, only for a short time.

"A girl?" he heard his mother ask.

"That's what he fucking said," Anton muttered. "Give me that, would you?"

"God, you're such a prick when you want to be," Viviana snapped.

"But I'm your prick, baby. And you love it."

"Love something about it."

Demyan cringed ten ways to Sunday. "You two are disgusting."

"No one asked for your opinion, Demyan," Anton replied derisively.

"Anton, what are you doing?" Viviana asked.

"Calling Ivan."

Demyan was stuck between amusement and annoyance. He placed his cell to the bed and turned on the speaker so Gia could hear the madness right along with him. She rolled her eyes and waved her own phone before turning it on speaker, too.

Shouts of unintelligible excitement rang out from her call. Then, both Ivan and Anton could be heard picking up the call for each other.

"It's a girl," Demyan's father said, laughing. "And you owe me a grand, man."

"I didn't agree to that bet, Anton!"

"Did so. Pay up, fucker."

Demyan shook his head in disbelief. Eva was chattering away about names and Viviana was saying something about Ana needing to be informed. Their families were insane. The brilliant smile playing on Gia's lips caught Demyan's attention like the ray of happiness it was.

He spoke to Ivan the week before. His father was right about what he said to Demyan a couple of months ago at his birthday party. He was a good man. A Bratva raised man, sure, but a good one where it counted. Ivan gave his permission, and it finally felt like the right time. He didn't have a ring, though. There wasn't any time for him to pick one out, but he didn't think Gia would mind. Gia met his gaze, her grin growing at the volcano of noise ringing through the phones. He couldn't think of a better time, really.

"I love you," she whispered.

Demyan smiled right back. "I know. Me, too. Marry me, Gia."

Both phones went silent as her jaw fell slack.

Gia blinked. "What?"

"I want you to marry me."

Gia reached over and ended both phone calls as she stared at Demyan. Not five seconds later, both phones starting vibrating with calls. They both ignored them.

33

"Why did you turn the phones off?" Demyan asked warily.

Had he made the wrong choice? Marriage had always been a sticky topic with Gia, partly because of their young age, her independence, and what would be Demyan's future in the Bratva.

"It shouldn't matter, you know," Demyan said, keeping his gaze locked on hers. "I know you worry about what might happen to me or whatever. I get you don't want feds knocking down our doors and searching our house someday if something goes wrong.

"And I know you don't want to be some pretty little mob wife playing her part, but none of that should matter, Gia. I love you. I'm always going to love you whether you're my wife or not. But, I'd really like it if you would be. I've wanted to marry you since I was five-years-old and figured out why my mother wore a ring on her finger that matched my father's."

"Stop rambling," Gia said.

"Okay."

"I hung up the phones because I didn't want anyone to think my answer was based on the pressure of others listening in."

Demyan's heart started beating again.

"Yes, Demyan, I'll marry you."

Chapter Four

Ana

"What do you think?" Cavan asked.

Ana tossed her bag onto the couch and turned a wide circle in the open loft, taking in the view from the windows. "It's really nice. Quiet."

"I thought so."

"So, hey, we're having a baby shower and engagement party for Demyan and his fiancée tomorrow. Would you want to come with me?" Ana asked, glancing at Cavan over her shoulder.

The look on his face said he didn't. She wasn't surprised.

"Not really."

Cavan was behind Ana in a second. He ran his hands down her sides as he placed a kiss on her neck. Ana shrugged out of his hold with as much grace as she could muster and put a safer distance between them. Cavan was attractive. Ana would be a goddamn liar if she pretended like parts of him didn't turn her on, but there was a lot about him that kept her at arm's length.

Like the fact he kept *her* at a distance.

Ana didn't know a whole lot about him, and after five dates over the span of a couple months, you'd think she would. He didn't like to talk about his family, she had yet to meet any of his friends, and this was the first time she had seen where he lived. Other than that, he didn't make any effort to let her in past his walls.

She was waiting for anything to give her an inclination why. At least something. But, nope, Cavan seemed to think his mystery was a desirable trait or some bullshit. Ana was getting tired of it.

Just because he was handsome and seemed nice didn't

mean Ana was going to jump in bed with someone she didn't know. That wasn't going to happen. Ever.

"Hey, what's that all about?" Cavan asked, raising a single brow.

Ana wet her lips, trying to figure out how to tell him to open up or back off. "I'm not in the market for a casual relationship, Cavan. Coffee, dinner, or a club is fine, but if you want to get any further than that with me, you're going to have to work a little harder for it. I didn't come up here with you to fuck."

Cavan scoffed. "I invited you to my loft, Ana. There isn't a whole hell of a lot to do in someone's place, you know. What else did you think I might want? I thought we were good and had something going on."

Ana bristled. "What we have going on is a few dates and your aloofness. I don't know anything about you, Cavan. If you want to get me into bed, take me further than the surface. Is that understood?"

Something unknown flashed in his eyes. "Yeah, I got it."

"Good."

Ana plucked her bag up from the couch, ready to leave. Cavan grabbed her wrist, stopping her. "Where are you going?"

"Back to my apartment," Ana replied. Cavan's grip on her tightened to an almost painful point and for a brief second, fear slipped through Ana's veins.

"Is there somebody else?" he asked, anger heating his tone. "Because I don't get why you keep pulling me in and then pushing me back. That shit is ridiculous. Nobody likes a tease, Ana."

A tease?

And when had they become anything at all? They weren't.

She glanced at his hand before saying, "Let me go."

Cavan did, instantly. "Sorry. Shit, Ana, I just—"

"I get it. We're on two different wavelengths. Give me a call when you get to mine or don't bother at all."

• • •

Large parties were not commonplace to the Avdonins. In fact, Ana's father preferred to keep people out of the privacy of their home. Birthdays and celebrations were quiet with a small attendance of guests. Especially if Anton and Viviana had the event at their house. Ana understood her parents reasoning, what with her father's status and the concern of an undercover official bleeding their way in.

Somehow, even though Ana knew Gia didn't want one, Demyan convinced his fiancée to allow both their parents to throw a co-ed baby shower mixed in with an engagement party. With two families inviting people plus Demyan's and Gia's guests, there was no room to move in the large Oceana home. The amount of people made Ana flustered.

Hell, Ana talked to people she didn't know from a hole in the ground.

Ana bet her father was going insane. But, Anton's weakness had always been Viviana. Ana had no doubts her mother used that to her advantage for this ... *thing*.

Ever since her brother announced the baby's gender and the two became engaged a month earlier, the party planning started. Ana didn't care for parties, but Gia and Demyan looked happy surrounded by people celebrating their joy. That was the most important thing.

Also, her soon-to-be sister-in-law definitely needed some merriment in her days. At twenty-eight weeks pregnant, Ana knew Gia was exhausted from teaching, her morning sickness hadn't abated, and now a wedding needed to be planned, too.

It was a lot.

Ana's gaze caught a blue-eyed stare from across the room. Koldan Vasin tipped his chin up in acknowledgment, amusement playing at the corner of his mouth. The oddest sensation washed over her skin as the man continued watching her. It tickled along her nerve endings like they were exposed to his attention, too.

She shouldn't have been surprised he was there. His

parents were, after all, and her father mentioned something about Koldan doing work for Adrik in New York. She didn't have the first clue what that meant and didn't want to know, either. Nonetheless, they hadn't come in contact with one another again since that dinner two months ago.

He sure looked at her like he wanted to talk to her, now.

Ana shivered and bit the inside of her cheek. Confusion didn't do her strange feelings justice. She didn't know Koldan, but what she did know, she wasn't entirely sure she liked. Ana wasn't stupid. She saw enough things over the years to know where she should and should not be sticking herself into.

Koldan was from Jersey and the only affiliation Ana's father had to Jersey was another Bratva family. A simple Internet check confirmed Ana's suspicions that the Vasin family was thoroughly mafia connected. Adrik was the goddamn boss, actually. Working for his father led Ana to the only conclusion there could be about Koldan: he was Bratva associated, too.

No fucking thanks.

So, why couldn't she shake his piercing stare still leveled entirely on her?

Ana gulped down a mouthful of red wine, gave Koldan one last glance, and then made her way through the throng of people milling between rooms. She needed space, or at the very least, some air to breathe.

The front step seemed as good of a place as any. Ana grabbed her sweater from the closet, tugged it on and slipped outside before one of her parents noticed her leaving. The coolness of the mid-October air felt refreshing compared to the claustrophobic heat inside the home. Resting her back to the brick wall of the house, she downed the rest of her wine in one drink and closed her eyes.

"It feels like ants inside a farm in there," came a dark, honeyed voice from her left.

Ana jumped with a squeak, her eyes flying wide open as the wine glass fell from her hand. It shattered across the decorative steps of the entryway. "Shit."

Koldan cocked a brow. "I didn't realize you knew those kinds of words."

"I beg your pardon?" Ana asked.

"Shit. I didn't realize you knew how to say a word like that."

"What in the hell is that supposed to mean?"

"Oh, there's another one," he said. "I almost feel like I should mark it down or something."

Her annoyance perked. "If you came out here to poke fun at me for your amusement, feel free to waltz right back inside the house before you really piss me off."

Koldan's grin grew. "Are you as beautiful when you're angry as you are when you're playing the good little girl for the public?"

Ana blinked, her mouth popping open audibly. She felt both offended and entertained at the same time. How was that even possible? "I don't remember you being this much of an asshole two months ago at dinner."

"I was making nice, kind of like you were," Koldan explained. "Seeing you today with all the people, fake smile plastered on and a blank stare, it kind of makes me wonder."

Don't poke the bear, Ana thought. She never was any good at listening to her inner voice. "Wonder what, Koldan?"

"Is this really who you are? I don't know. What are you like outside of your parents' view?"

Again, Ana gaped, stunned speechless.

"My sister," Koldan continued, "... she's wild as fuck, but you wouldn't know it when my dad's around. Adrik spoiled her like nothing else growing up. All she has to do is bat her lashes at him and he's fucking putty. He thinks she's going to settle down with some connected man like any good mob wife because she's got our father living in delusions. It's never going to happen, you know. Sofia, she doesn't want to be a guy's one girl, she's the type who gets labeled the other girl. Get what I mean?"

"Did you just call your sister a whore?" Ana asked sharply.

"Hell, no. My sister gets no judgment from me as far as her preferences for dating, or lack thereof depending on how you want to look at it. I just say it like I see it. Sofia gets to be and do whatever the fuck she wants in my book, including men. It's her right. What I meant, was that who our father sees and who the rest of the world sees are two entirely different people. She's not upfront with her motives and that shit unsettles me in a way I can't explain."

Ana crossed her arms, feeling a bit unsettled herself. "Why are you telling me this at all?"

"You've got me curious, Ana. You're beautiful, for one thing. Don't fault me for looking. Unfortunately, when you draw my eye, it means I'm going to notice other things, too. Like that sweet but fake smile to the crowd. Or when your back is against a wall while you toss down a half a glass of wine before you make a beeline for the door. Being curious means I might want to know more about you, but if that also means learning two completely different people, I would like to be warned before I even tried."

"Wow," Ana mouthed, not sure what else to say.

Koldan shrugged. "I'm not in the business of hiding my intentions, the things I do, or who I am. I don't make excuses for any of it, either. Honesty gets a man everywhere."

It sure did, in most cases.

Ana couldn't help but like the fact Koldan was as frank and blunt as he was. To Ana, because she lived in a world where sometimes feelings and opinions were left at the door, this man's boldness was appealing.

And *frightening*.

But, hey, if he wanted to play the honesty game, Ana could do that, too. "Why are you here, anyway?"

"Work."

Ana nodded, passing him a look. "Yeah, that's what I thought."

"If you want a better answer, *krasivyy*, ask a better question."

Point taken.

"Fine. What kind of work?"

"Anton and Adrik have an arrangement that's been ongoing for years. It works for them, I guess. Regardless, there's been a few issues getting shipments ready to transport at the time they're supposed to be rolling out due to a new crew working the docks, so here I am to make sure everything is smooth sailing for the next couple of months. Or, however long it takes to work all the kinks out."

Ana's brow furrowed. "Shipments?"

"Oh, come on, Ana. You're telling me you don't know the kinds of things your father is involved in?"

"No, I know," she said quietly, refusing to meet his gaze. "I just don't know how it all works or whatever."

"Shipments, the product making the money. Whatever might be selling hot like candy on the streets, it's coming off those ships in crates."

"Oh."

"Yeah," Koldan said simply. "Bothers you, doesn't it?"

"What you do?" Ana asked back.

"That's what I said. Disgust is written all over your face."

Ana mulled his words over, deciding to choose her own carefully. "I have a trust fund coming to me when I'm thirty, a Mercedes bought by my father, a fully paid education, and a monthly allowance paying for my apartment and needs while letting me focus on school instead of work."

Koldan's expression didn't change a bit. "What's your point?"

"How hypocritical of me would it be to say I don't approve of what you do for a living, yet know the things I have are paid for with the same kind of money?"

"Nobody said you had to approve of it. Nobody is asking for your permission, Ana."

"No shit," Ana muttered, blowing out a huff of air.

"You missed *my* point this time," he said, winking. "It's your choice what you want to do now, okay. Your car? It probably showed up one day with a bow on it. Your schooling, apartment, and allowance? That's what parents are

41

supposed to do—take care of their kids and provide for them so they can be better and have better than what they did. That trust fund? Spend it or give it all away.

"You don't need *their* approval because it's yours. You don't have to like what I do, Ana. It's my choice. You have your own choices to make. Simple as that. And if when making those choices, you refuse certain things because of the root at which they came from, that's all on you. Nobody cares because nobody here is looking for permission. They do what they want to do, you do what you want to do."

Huh. Ana never thought of it that way before.

"Besides," Koldan drawled, grinning roguishly. "What I do for a living doesn't stop me from having the same kind of interests and feelings as you, Ana. My hands might be a little dirtier than yours, but they dress up nice all the same. By the way, good deflection. I'm impressed, but not stupid or easily distracted."

"What deflection?"

"Is there two of you to learn, or just the one?"

Ana gestured at the front door. "Maybe if you weren't so busy staring at me in there, you might have noticed my parents are sporting the same attitude I have. Be good, smile, and get it done with. My family, we don't have parties like this. We never have because my parents are too private and distrustful of outsiders. But, it's not about us, right? It's about Demyan and Gia. So—"

"You be good, smile, and get it done with," Koldan interrupted softly. "I get it."

"Do you?" Ana asked.

"Sure, just the same way Adrik forces me to the Temple though I'd rather chew glass."

Ana giggled. It was completely inappropriate, but she did. "Nice. You're honest. I like that."

"Speaking of being honest, what are you doing for the next couple of hours?"

"You're looking at it, Koldan."

He gestured at the house. "Yeah, but you don't really want

to be here and that house is so full no one will notice you're gone."

Ana swallowed the thickness building in her throat, her nerves taking over. "Are you asking me out right now?"

"Absolutely, *right* now," Koldan murmured. "If this party isn't your kind of thing, I'd like for you to show me what is. What's holding you back?"

Nothing, really.

"A boyfriend?" he asked.

Ana considered Cavan though only briefly. Really, she thought of him for Koldan's sake more than her own. The guy wanted truthfulness, after all. Koldan was nothing like Cavan who couldn't or wouldn't let her in. She preferred Koldan's no-nonsense attitude and straightforward intentions to Cavan's distance and evasiveness.

"You want all the cards face up, right?" Ana asked. Koldan nodded. "I don't play games. I've been seeing someone I met a couple of months ago, but it's not serious, we're not a couple, and we're not intimately involved. Actually, we've gone on a few dates and he sometimes shows up after my classes to have coffee."

"Anyone else?"

"I don't do casual sex, if that's what you're asking."

Koldan smirked. "It was, so thanks."

"I'm not an easy lay, I won't do a one-night stand, and my father is a mob boss with a short temper and a collection of guns. Still want to take me out?" Ana asked.

"Like crazy."

Chapter Five

Demyan

The elbow jamming into Demyan's side was really getting annoying.

"Demyan Avdonin, I swear to God if you don't pick up that fucking phone of yours I'm going to smash it into the wall. I have to be up at five to get ready for work!"

Why was it that every time he began to fall asleep, something or someone was waking him up? It was starting to get ridiculous. Demyan turned to his side in an attempt to avoid another bony appendage ramming into his kidney, but instead, Gia simply smacked his bare back with her opened palm. The sting radiated over his skin like painful little fireworks

"Shit, ow," Demyan hissed in the dark, finally semi-awake. "That hurt, *katyonak*."

"You sleep like the dead. Pick up the phone or the next one is going to knock you onto the floor. Don't test me. The couch isn't comfortable, babe."

Despite her obvious aggravation at him, Demyan chuckled. Gia was terribly sexy when she was angry. One of the better perks of having a fiery woman for his best friend and lover. "Love it when you get nasty."

"Ugh, shut up. You're such a pig."

"You love it."

"Pick up the phone!"

Groaning, Demyan rolled over in the bed and skimmed his hand over the nightstand to find his ringing phone. He didn't bother to check the caller ID as he fell back into the bed. Putting his hand on Gia's rounded stomach to feel his daughter's movements, he answered the call.

"Yeah, *allo*."

"Demyan, I need your help."

"Ana?" Demyan sat up straight in the bed at the terror in his sister's voice. "Ana, what's wrong?"

"Can you let me in?" she asked barely above a breath. "Please, Demyan."

"You're at my place?"

Why would Ana be there?

"Yes, just *please* come open the door, Demyan."

Fear seemed to saturate her every word. A cold chill ran down Demyan's spine. "Yeah, yeah … shit, just give me a few minutes. I'm fucking indecent and in bed with Gia. Are you okay?"

"No," Ana said, crying low. "I'm not."

"All right. One minute, then," Demyan muttered, pushing up from the bed to stand. Gia followed, not asking any questions.

"Please don't hang up the phone."

Demyan froze as he reached for his slacks hanging over the bedpost. He had never heard his little sister so entirely shaken and afraid before. She was stubborn as hell, sassy, and quick. They didn't always get along, and maybe they weren't close, but that didn't mean he was oblivious to her good traits. The girl on the other end of the call was not the Ana he knew.

"Demyan?" Gia asked.

He swallowed hard, panic welling in his gut. He couldn't answer Gia because his focus was entirely on his sister. "Thirty seconds, Ana, okay?"

"Just don't hang up the phone," she whispered.

"I won't."

Demyan wasted no time yanking on his slacks. He tossed a silk dress shirt to Gia for her to put on. In a blink, he was jogging through the apartment, turning on every light as he went with the phone still pressed to his ear. Ana didn't say a word, but her soft sobbing sliced him straight down to the fucking bone.

"I'm coming, Ana," he said, wanting her to know.

"Okay."

Demyan flicked off the chain and turned the deadbolt before throwing open the front door. The phone dropped from his hand to the hardwood floor as he took in the sight of his baby sister. Her usually curly black hair was a mess, her makeup was smudged and ruined. Tears streaked down her face. Her short black dress was crumpled and disheveled and her entire body was shaking all over. She clenched her phone in one hand, held her bag to her chest with the other, and seemed to be literally trying to turn in on herself.

Worst of all, she wouldn't meet his stare.

Demyan lurched forward out of instinct, needing to protect his sister from whatever had turned her into what was standing in front of him. A full-body flinch took over Ana when Demyan held her wet, messy face in his palms, forcing her to look at him. Redness and puffiness littered her eyes. Teeth mark fissures cut across her bottom lip. Fingerprint bruises marred the left side of her jaw.

"Oh my God, Ana," Demyan managed to croak. "Look at you."

Ana sobbed. "I'm sorry, Demyan. I didn't know where else to go."

"No. Christ, it's—" He stopped himself from saying fine, because clearly she was not. "Never mind, you know you can always come to me, Ana. *Always.*"

She nodded jerkily, more tears falling down to his hands. "I know."

Demyan surveyed the bruises on Ana's jaw one more time, rolling his thumb along the line of marks. Who had done this to his sister? Why would they do this to her? He didn't like the looks of her injury added on to the mess of her clothes.

"You know you can tell me anything, right?" Demyan said, keeping his gaze locked on hers. "Anything, Ana. I'll do whatever you need me to, but you need to tell me what happened."

Ana whimpered a terrible sound before her knees gave out and she fell into his arms. Demyan didn't hesitate to pick her up in a cradled embrace. She buried her face into his chest and bawled harder. The force of her sobs shook them both. Gia, who had stayed quiet behind Demyan, moved aside to let him pass into the living-room.

"Gia, close and lock the door, babe."

"Yeah, okay," Gia replied with a shake to her tone.

Demyan deposited Ana on the couch, kneeling down in front of her to fix her messy hair and clean her face. It didn't help much, considering the tears kept coming every time he wiped them away. Her muscles felt as tight as a coiled wire ready to snap. He heard her teeth grinding beneath her clenched jaw. Every time he touched her, she folded inwards to get away from his hands.

"Ana, look at me," Demyan ordered.

She wouldn't.

The sick feeling pummeling his insides was a killer.

"Demyan, do you need me to call somebody?" Gia asked.

Ana flew into a round of hysterics. "No, no, no! You can't, Demyan, you *can't!*"

"Calm down," Demyan whispered, his hands ghosting over Ana's face to wipe away the wetness. "Ana, if something really bad happened, I need to call Papa. He'll fucking kill me if I don't. Okay?"

"No," Ana wheezed, her eyes flying wide and her hands grabbing his wrists so hard her nails cut into his skin. "Please, you can't call Papa."

"Ana—"

"Please don't tell him. He can't know. I ... I don't want him to know."

"Know what?" Demyan asked. "Just tell me what happened."

"It doesn't matter," Ana said, shaking her head.

"It goddamn well does."

"No, just promise me you won't call anybody, Demyan. I needed a safe place to sleep, that's all."

Demyan's heart was cracking and anxiety drove through his body like a wrecking ball. None of his sister's words made any sense and by the way she appeared, something awful had gone down with her. Tears welled in Ana's gaze as she stared at him, silently begging.

"Okay," Demyan agreed quietly. "I won't call, but you need to tell me what happened."

Ana choked on her cries, her hands fisting into her lap. "I just want to sleep. Please let me sleep, Demyan."

Over his shoulder, Demyan gave Gia a pleading look. His lover didn't seem to have an answer for him, either. Not that his mind wasn't drawing its own conclusions because it was. Unfortunately, the only thing Demyan's thoughts were coming up with was practically fucking unthinkable.

Disgusting. Devastating. Horrible.

Not his sister. Not Ana.

"I'm so tired," Ana said, gaining his attention again.

Demyan's heart broke a little more. "Okay, you can sleep. You want a blanket or something?"

Ana nodded and he stood to go find what she needed, but Gia was already making her way to the spare room where the linens were kept. He sat down on the recliner across from his sister, stunned and unsure of his next move. By the time Gia got back, Ana was curled up in the fetal position on the couch using her arm as a pillow.

Demyan couldn't stop watching the distant stare his sister sported. She wanted to sleep, but she wasn't closing her eyes. It was only when Gia gasped quietly and the blanket she held fell over the arm of the couch did his attention focus elsewhere.

Straight to where Gia was staring.

Nausea swept Demyan under the current and rage hit him like a punch in the gut. The black dress Ana wore was club-style and popular to her age. Short, slinky material and tight. Demyan hadn't noticed before because the fabric rode low enough across her thighs to hide it. The marks on Ana's face were nothing compared to the palm and finger bruises curving around her inner thighs.

Like someone had forced them open.

Jesus fucking Christ.

God, *no.*

• • •

Demyan didn't sleep. Not a fucking wink. He didn't leave his sister's sleeping side. He all but forced Gia to go back to bed well after three in the morning. When she got up at her regular time to get ready for work, he ordered his pregnant fiancée back to sleep. She had tossed a glance at Ana still and somber on the couch and didn't argue.

Now, after she slept and could think, Gia stood toe to toe with him, angry.

"You have to call someone or the proper authorities. It's your responsibility as her brother, Demyan!"

Demyan's lips drew a thin line. "First off, she doesn't want me to call. Did you see the same thing I did last night, Gia? She's clearly terrified of my father finding out, for whatever reason. I need to calm her down first and—"

"And the longer you wait, the less she remembers and evidence gets contaminated. You're letting her shower, for Christ's sake!"

"Because she wants to. It was her choice and I don't blame her for wanting to."

"She shouldn't shower, Demyan."

"I'm sorry, Gia, but even when I do call someone, it will not be to the police. We can't involve cops. Ever. If past experience is anything to go on, the officials are more interested in what they can get from a victim about the family they're involved in rather than the attack. I know it sucks, but that's how it is. I have to keep my family safe. We'll take care of it just as soon as I get a name from her."

"Take care of it," Gia echoed.

"Yes. I know you don't like that."

"I don't, but it's the only option she has for retribution, so." Gia shuddered, but her gaze steeled. "Promise me, even if it takes months to find out, you will take care of it,

49

Demyan."

Speechless at her demand, Demyan could only nod.

The knock on the apartment door interrupted their conversation from going further. Demyan knew it was Koldan, as he called the guy earlier in the morning to pick up something for him Ana might need. They worked the docks together. Koldan was solid to Demyan in the way he would keep his mouth shut. Plus, Demyan needed someone uninvolved with his father to do some poking around if Ana wouldn't talk.

"Can you go check on her, get her something to wear, and make sure she's comfortable while I deal with that?" Demyan asked.

"Sure, babe," Gia said softly. "Are you okay?"

"Not really."

"Yeah, I didn't think so."

Gia leaned up and kissed his cheek before leaving him alone. Demyan answered the door with a blank expression, not wanting to show his anger or panic. Koldan stood on the other side, looking inside a pharmacy bag he held and chuckling.

"Hey," Demyan said.

"Morning." Koldan glanced up with his brow lifted, laughing. "Man, you do know your girl is way too far along to be using this shit, right?"

Demyan understood Koldan was joking, but it didn't stop the growl of warning forming in the back of his throat. Immediately, Koldan's chuckles quieted and his amusement disappeared. "Whoa, Demyan. Chill. What did I miss?"

Stepping back, Demyan waved at the entranceway behind him. "Get inside."

Koldan did, closing the door behind him and handing the pharmacy bag over. He gave Demyan a once over before asking, "Seriously, what the fuck is up? You look ready to kill."

So, maybe Demyan still had issues with hiding his emotions.

Demyan didn't answer Koldan. Instead, he pulled out the rectangular box from the pharmacy bag and read the fine print on the side.

Plan B. Christ. It made him sick just having to look at it and consider his sister might need what was in the box.

"You can just walk in and pick this shit up, huh?"

Koldan nodded. "Basically. Pharmacist gives you a run down on how to use it properly and the window of time it's effective."

"And how long is that?" Demyan asked.

"Anywhere from seventy-two hours to one-hundred-twenty, but the sooner it's taken after unprotected sex, the better."

"All right, then."

Koldan cleared his throat, looking uncomfortable. "I didn't take you for the kind to mess around on your girl, Demyan."

Demyan's head jerked up, his eyes narrowing. "I didn't and I'm not. Something bad went down last—"

"Oh, God," Ana cried from somewhere behind Demyan.

Demyan turned fast on his heel to face his panicking sister. She was looking right at Koldan who had suddenly turned as stiff as a board beside Demyan. There was something about the way Ana stared at Koldan that set Demyan's nerves on edge. Not in a bad way, but like he somehow missed something important between the two.

Koldan took a step further into the apartment, his gaze snapping back and forth to the marks littering Ana's face and the box in Demyan's hand. It wasn't hard to put two and two together. A shuddering exhale escaped Koldan and it sounded almost painful.

"I thought you blew me off," Koldan said, taking yet another step toward Ana.

"No," Ana whispered. "I was leaving to meet up with you."

"Oh, *krasivyy.*"

Demyan watched in stunned silence as his sister broke

into pieces all over again. Only this time, it wasn't him who rushed forward to hold her together and she didn't flinch away from Koldan's hands like she had Demyan's.

Chapter Six

Ana

Ana didn't want to cry, but telling her mind to cooperate with her wishes was impossible.

Koldan held her tight, absorbing her trembling and shielding her face with his embrace. Ana thought it odd she was okay with him so close, but he hadn't given her any reason not to trust him. They'd only gone out three times together since the party two weeks earlier, but it had been enough for her to know she was interested in more with Koldan.

"Tell me who did this to you," Koldan said in her ear. "Tell me, *krasivyy*."

Memories she had forced back from the night before slammed into her. It hit her like a ton of bricks to the chest. Fingers digging into her jaw to hold her still. Her teeth biting her bottom lip and blood seeping into her mouth. A hand at her thighs … pain.

Cavan.

Ana gagged at his name alone. The toast and juice she forced down earlier came back up violently. She barely managed to turn out of Koldan's hold in time to find the small wastebasket beside the couch.

"Shit," she heard Demyan hiss.

On her knees, Ana shook from the force of her vomiting. Koldan was behind her instantly, his one hand sweeping her hair back to the nape of her neck while his other arm wrapped around her middle.

"He … he called me," Ana managed to get out, her balled fists vibrating against the floor as her teeth chattered.

"When?" Koldan asked.

Somehow, she calmed her nerves enough to talk.

"Before I was going to leave for the club to meet you." Ana sobbed brokenly as Koldan shushed a soothing sound in her ear, rocking her gently. She had to keep talking, though. If she didn't, the fear burning through her veins would keep her silent forever. "I told him to leave me alone unless he figured out where he wanted to go with me. When he called, he said he wanted to come over to my apartment to talk, and I thought ..."

Koldan's thumb rolled softly along her racing pulse point. "What, Ana?"

"I thought I could tell him, then. I didn't want to date him, or see him or anything. Because you and me, you know. B-but he already knew."

Koldan stilled. "About me?"

Ana cried harder, nodding frantically. "Said he found me with you. Saturday, the club."

"Twisted," Koldan said faintly, naming the club in question.

"He saw us when we ..."

Ana didn't want to finish her sentence, humiliation and shame filling her to the brim. She didn't have to, anyway. The way Koldan tensed behind her, she knew he understood what she was getting at.

At that club, Koldan pushed Ana into a dark corner and kissed her until she was breathless, wide-eyed, and already half in lust and half in love with him. His hands wandered over her figure with a clear intent to imprint every one of her curves to memory by touch alone. He watched her under dim lighting with a gaze so intense it heated every drop of blood in her body to a boil.

That night, Ana would have tossed out everything she thought she believed in for Koldan had he let her. But, he didn't. What he did was drop her off at her apartment with a tender kiss and a promise to take her out the next Sunday.

That's where she was supposed to be last night, not ... where she ended up.

Ana shivered even though she wasn't cold. The memory

of Koldan which had kept her grinning a private smile all week seemed tainted, somehow. Her body felt so dirty even though she spent an hour in the shower. She suddenly wanted to jump back into one with the water turned on as hot as it would go.

The panic and disgust welled. She panted out gasps of burning air as the urge to vomit plowed its way up again.

"Ana, it's okay, take deep breaths." Koldan's arm tightened around her midsection, rooting her in place and stopping her from giving in to the need she felt to run and hide. "This ... guy, was he the one you were seeing, but it wasn't anything serious?"

She bobbed her head once to confirm his question. Tears streaked lines down her face, dripping onto the floor. "He was so angry. So, so angry about seeing me doing what I wouldn't with him. I didn't ... he hadn't ever before ... I never thought to worry or have someone—"

"You shouldn't have needed to worry at all. I need you to give me a name," Koldan said so quietly she barely heard him. "Just give me his name, Ana."

She couldn't. The words Cavan threatened her with were imprinted into her memory.

Do you think your family scares me, Ana? You should meet mine. There wouldn't be one of you left when we were done.

Who had she gotten herself mixed up with? Ana didn't know, but Cavan's strangeness and secrecy suddenly make a lot more sense if he had his own crime affiliation he needed to hide. How could she be stupid enough to put her family in danger like that?

"Ana," Koldan said sharply, yanking her out of her thoughts. "Breathe!"

Hadn't she been?

Apparently not, because she sucked in air like it was water and she was dying of thirst.

"I can't tell you," Ana cried. "I *can't*."

"Maybe not right now," Koldan agreed. "But, you are going to tell me eventually."

Koldan managed to convince Ana to get up and sit on the couch. Demyan and Gia moved around the two in silence, taking away the wastebasket and setting a full glass of water on the coffee table. Koldan stayed kneeled at her feet, his eyes locked on hers while he helped her to sip from the glass as her hands were shaking too hard.

Demyan came to sit on the other end of the couch. This time, she managed not to flinch away from his proximity. The saddened, worried look he sported ratcheted up the shame she still felt.

Ana hadn't meant to be frightened of her brother the night before. She worried he would think badly of her for what happened. Or worse, not believe her at all. Of course, she knew better than that inside, but the way the terror acted like a poison and her mind went into anxiety overload, it was the only thing she could think of.

Demyan leaned over and set a white box beside Ana's thigh. "Here, if you need this, you should take it sooner rather than later. I'm ... going to go check on Gia. If you want me, just say my name. Okay?"

Ana couldn't move. Emotions suffocated her. The box resting beside her was taunting, frightening, and horrifying all at once.

For the first time, Koldan looked truly uncomfortable and not just disturbed, concerned, or angry like before. She could tell he was chewing his unspoken question over.

"We like the cards face up," he said quietly.

Ana blew out a breath, hiding her face from his view by tipping her chin down. "We do."

"Do you need to take that, *krasivyy*?"

She did.

Koldan helped when she fumbled with the package to get it open and said nothing when she choked the pill down.

• • •

Ana stared at the iPod resting in her lap. Her mind swam in a

56

haze.

She was so lost. A week after her attack, she still felt as raw as the moment Cavan left her crying on her apartment floor. There was nothing that could get the feel of him off her. No amount of water, soap, or scrubbing.

God knew she tried to get him away. She couldn't. He was inside her fucking *head*.

Debilitated and used. She couldn't sleep, eat, and her thoughts were plagued with … him. Her own home—her apartment—didn't have that same safe aura it once did. Even the thought of going back had bile rising in her tightening throat. She skipped classes all week, unable to focus or breathe with strangers around.

Cavan did this to her.

Made her feel ruined, weak, and isolated.

So fucking alone.

In a room full of people, she was still alone.

"Earth to Ana."

Ana looked at her mother sitting beside her. "Yeah, Ma?"

Viviana frowned, tilting her head to the side as she regarded her daughter. "What's up with you?"

"Nothing, Ma."

"I said your name five times before you finally noticed."

"Sorry. I've uh … got a lot on my plate with college."

Her mother leaned back into the couch. "Oh, really?"

"Yeah."

Ana pleaded in her head for her mother to drop the topic. Viviana was far too observant when it came to her children and was liable to notice something was off if Ana couldn't somehow divert her attention.

"College, huh?" Viviana asked quietly.

"I just said that, Ma."

"Well, if you have a lot going on, why did you skip classes today?"

Anton poked his head into the living room, interrupting the conversation. "Vine, where's that suit jacket you picked up from the cleaners?"

Ana was grateful for her father's intrusion. She took the chance to shove her earbuds for her iPod into her ears. She didn't turn the iPod on but hoped her mother wouldn't notice and leave her alone, anyway.

"Hanging on the back door of the laundry room," Viviana said, eyeing Ana from the side.

Ana pretended not to notice.

Her father cleared his throat, making Ana flinch on the inside. "Something going on I need to know about, baby?"

"I don't know," Viviana replied. "Maybe."

Unsettled that her parents noticed her restless nervousness and distraction, Ana stood from the couch without a word. She grabbed the messenger bag she dropped earlier and slung it over her shoulder, tugging the earbuds out in the process before shoving the iPod into her pack.

"Ana, where are you going? I thought we were—"

"I have to go, Ma. Sorry."

"But—"

"I have to go," Ana snapped.

"Ana, don't talk to your mother like that. Apologize."

She ignored her father's chastising, moving to leave.

"Hey, you wait right there just a goddamn minute," Anton demanded.

When Ana slipped past her father's large form to get to the hallway, he reached out to grab her arm. Ana jerked back from the touch like she'd been burned. Anton's spine straightened, his gaze flicking over his daughter's face. Ana knew she probably looked like a scared cat ready to run.

She needed to get as far away from her parents as she could or else her cracks would keep showing. They'd split and open up until her flaws and mistakes were out there for them to see. If she cried, they would *know*.

Ana didn't want them to.

"I'm sorry," Ana said, holding back tears. "Please let me leave."

Anton, seeming stunned, stepped aside silently to let her pass.

Her father would never hurt her. Even when she was a bratty little child, he never once put his hands on her in anger. He loved her.

Ana was, and always had been, his princess. She did no wrong in her father's eyes.

How would he feel about her if he found out what happened?

• • •

"Thank you for meeting me," Ana said, trying to smile but failing.

Koldan sipped on a to-go cup of coffee, shrugging under the weight of his leather jacket. "Wasn't doing much, anyway."

"Liar. When I called, there was so much noise in the background, I couldn't hear you."

"Doesn't mean it was important to me, so it's better for me to move on to what is," he replied like it didn't make a difference.

Ana didn't miss his unspoken words.

Other things weren't important to him. She was.

Koldan tipped his head in the direction of her coffee. "Drink before it goes cold, *krasivyy*."

Ana's hands were warmed by the coffee. The late October air chilled every other part of her. They could have stayed inside the coffee shop after they purchased their drinks, but the amount of people inside sent Ana's anxiety swimming thick.

Did they know when they looked at her?

Could they see her invisible damage?

Because sure, the bruises were gone and the ache had left, but inside … she was broken.

"Hey," Koldan murmured, gazing at her with an intensity that seemed to dig right down into her soul. "I lost you there for a second."

Ana barked out a laugh. Pulling her legs up to rest her feet on the bench under her backside, she placed the cup to the side and sighed. "You're not the only one."

"What's going on, Ana? Talk to me. You call me in a panic, ask me to meet up with you, and then stare dazed at your hands. I'm fine with doing that, too. Watching you watch nothing, I mean. If that's what you need, cool shit, but I don't think it is. Come on, just talk."

Sucking in another gulp of air, Ana explained her earlier close call with her parents. Koldan stayed silent through her tale, worry and sadness dancing in his gaze while his shoulders grew tense.

"They're going to pick up on your depression, Ana," he said when she finished. "They're your parents and they love you. They raised you, so trust that they know when something's not right with their kid."

Ana blinked, confused. "I'm not … depressed."

Koldan cleared his throat, setting his own coffee down and resting his clasped hands between his knees. "Depression is more than suicide, you know. Most people, that's the only thing they consider when depression gets tossed out there. It's way more than that. Sometimes you just don't want to talk, move, or even think. You hurt, physically and emotionally. You're drained—exhausted. Irritability walks hand in hand with your sadness. For no reason other than the fact you couldn't be anything else, you're stuck in a cloudy haze that won't clear."

"Depression," Ana echoed.

"You're still raw," he continued. "It's only been a week, but it's not going to get better if you keep putting on a brave face while the fears eat away at you on the inside. What you need is support and professional care, Ana, or it's only going to get worse. You should tell your parents so they can help you."

Horror squeezed Ana's throat like a noose. "I can't."

"Listen, no one is saying you have to name a name though I really wish you would. What I'm trying to get you to understand is even admitting to them an attack happened might be beneficial in more ways than you know. Therapy or—"

"I can't tell them." Ana's rebuttal came out fierce as she stood from the bench to end the conversation and leave. He followed suit but kept a safe distance between them. Ana was grateful.

"Don't run away from me right now," Koldan said, looking as though he wanted to reach out to her. "I'm only trying to help."

"I know."

She did, really, but it was still hard.

"Why won't you tell your parents so they can love and care for you?"

"Because, I am not that kind of girl," Ana whispered, finally letting the tears escape. "They didn't raise me jump into bed with whoever caught my eye. I don't want them thinking I somehow put myself into a position where the attack happened because of my stupidity."

"They wouldn't," Koldan said, something unknown darkening his voice. "There's a huge difference between being disappointed because a parent believes their daughter doesn't respect her body and victim-blaming her for an attack that wasn't her fault. This shit right here—" Koldan waved at her. "—is victim-blaming at its best. And you're the fucking victim! A woman doesn't ask to be raped, Ana. It doesn't matter if she's walking down a dark alley naked and drunk off her ass, she's not giving permission for a man to rape her. Don't you get that?"

"I—"

"No, hear me right now. This wasn't your fault. Say it."

Ana's throat closed, keeping her silent.

"Say it," Koldan demanded. "It wasn't your fault."

"It wasn't my fault," she repeated above a breath.

Ana wiped the wetness from her face with the sleeves of her sweater. Koldan took a hesitant step forward with his arms open. She let him swallow her in the embrace.

"Thank you," Ana said.

"Shit, no. Don't thank me for that. It had to get out there, you know?"

"It's just hard because he took a really important choice away from me. I'd never—" Ana clamped her mouth shut, refusing to admit what almost spilled out. Apparently, what she had said was enough.

Koldan stilled. "Never had sex."

"No. I did other things, but never that. He took it away from me. It's like I'm ... damaged goods or something. I know it's not true, but that's how I feel right now."

"Christ." Koldan sighed as he tried to make Ana look at him again. When she wouldn't, his gentle hands held her chin up so she couldn't look away. "I get what you're trying to say, but I don't agree. Virginity is more than breaking a hymen. A woman is worth more than her hymen, for that matter. I don't know what else to say so you understand who you are is far more than this one moment and what happened, Ana. It will get better, it doesn't define you and you're not ruined."

Ana smiled honestly for the first time in a week. "What are you, some kind of male feminist?"

"No, I'm just a man." Koldan shrugged and added, "According to my father, a little free-spirited and intense, but a good one."

"I agree with him."

"Yeah, don't ever tell him that. He'll never let you live it down."

Ana snorted. "Okay."

"And, please consider telling your parents."

"I will."

Feeling better than she had all week, Ana stayed silent and comfortable in Koldan's hug. When she looked over his shoulder to stare down the quiet street, her blood froze in her veins. A quiet whimper lodged in her throat.

Cavan.

He was making his way out of a specialty shop and didn't seem to notice her.

It didn't make a fucking difference. She noticed him. And

Koldan took notice of her immediate fear.

"Ana?"

She couldn't answer him. She couldn't even breathe.

Koldan turned to look and she knew what he was seeing. The only guy walking down the sidewalk toward a black SUV.

"Please tell me that's not him," Koldan said so low she strained to hear. Ana trembled, refusing to say a single word. "Do you know who he is?"

"C-cavan Dolan," Ana mumbled.

"Yeah, the nephew and only heir to Liam Dolan, Ana."

"W-what ... who?"

"The Irish mob boss Liam Dolan from Detroit. That's his nephew."

And her rapist.

Oh, God.

Chapter Seven

Demyan

"How the fuck do you know Cavan Dolan, huh? I didn't realize the Avdonins were doing business with the Irish mob! Do you realize how thick they are into human-trafficking? Adrik won't want any part of that shit, Demyan!"

Demyan stopped his trek to his car, unsure. Koldan's anger spilled into the phone like hot lava. "We're not."

"Oh? Funny, because—"

"No, shut the hell up," Demyan barked. "We're not involved with the Irish mob, Koldan. At all. We don't play with other organizations or families. Anton hasn't mixed business with anyone but Adrik since the mess with my mother's family. Remember who you're fucking talking to here, man."

Koldan all but snarled on the other end of the phone. "Cavan—"

"Showed up at my birthday party months ago. I didn't know who he was at first. I let that Irish bastard know to stay away from my family. We don't want any part of them around. We're not in the mood for friends."

"You really need to stop interrupting me."

"You need to learn some fucking respect!"

"Koldan?"

Ana's soft, scared voice on the other end of the call made Demyan squeeze his eyes closed. He wasn't entirely impressed by whatever his sister had going on with Adrik's son, but he kept his opinion to himself. Especially considering Koldan seemed to help and like his sister a lot.

Ana stayed at Demyan's place all week, so he had more than enough chances to see the two in action with one another. Ana talked when she wouldn't to anyone else.

Koldan listened. Sometimes the guy dropped by just to check up on her. She needed that more than she realized.

So yeah, Demyan kept his fucking mouth shut.

"What are you doing with Ana? You're supposed to be supervising those idiots down at the docks."

"None of your business," Koldan snapped.

"We both know it is," Demyan retorted hotly.

"Talking, asshole. Can I speak without you cutting in on me, now?"

"Whatever. I suggest you tread lightly."

"Where are you?" Koldan asked.

"Just got done my last class and was going home for a quick shower before I head down to meet up with you. Or, that's what I was doing. I don't know what you're doing, now, so I don't know what the fuck I'm doing. Why?"

"Cavan was it, man. Ana's attack—he's the one."

"Koldan, you promised!" Ana cried.

"I lied," he told her. "Please don't ask me to apologize for it, either, Ana."

Demyan blew out a harsh breath. "You're sure?"

"Oh, yeah," Koldan confirmed quietly. "Very."

Another thought passed through Demyan's mind. "Was he the guy she talked about seeing the last couple months?"

"Yep."

"Meet me at my apartment in thirty."

"Already on our way. It's not going to take you thirty minutes to drive here. What the hell?"

Demyan unlocked his car, tossed his bag inside before slamming it shut and locking it again. "I need to have a chat with Freddie."

"All right. In thirty, then."

Demyan ended the conversation without another word. A simple text to Freddie gave Demyan the guy's location on campus. Demyan jogged the fifteen-minute journey to find him. When he did, he grabbed Freddie by his jacket and shoved him roughly into the closest wall before the guy had a chance to react.

Freddie's hands flew up in surrender. "Whoa, Demyan. What the fuck, man?"

"Cavan Dolan, Freddie. That's what. Why was he messing around with my sister?"

Freddie didn't look like he had the first clue what Demyan was talking about. "The guy likes his females, so if he picked up Ana, I—"

Demyan slammed Freddie into the wall again, shutting him up. "He was seeing her for a good while after I warned him to stay away. Why?"

"I don't know. Would you let me go? You're freaking me out."

"Not until I'm done here. Did he know you were involved with me months ago when you brought him to my parents' home?"

"No, not until that day. What's wrong, Demyan?"

"How many other girls has he raped when they didn't give him what he wanted?"

Freddie's tense body slumped against the wall. "He raped Ana?"

"How many, Freddie?"

"I heard rumors about Detroit, but ... I thought that's just what they were."

"Where does he live?"

Freddie rattled off an address.

Demyan let him go, taking a step back to fix his jacket. "We didn't have this goddamn conversation. Got it?"

"Yeah, man. I got it."

• • •

Demyan spun the tip of the knife on the pad of his thumb. A tiny drop of blood gathered at and he wiped it away on the arm of his jacket. Coldness settled in his gut while rage burned white-hot through the rest of his body.

Silence stilled his mind.

Tilting his head back against the wall, Demyan overlooked

the view the tall glass windows of Cavan Dolan's loft offered. The windowsill bench had been Demyan's seat for three hours. Minimal movement, no thoughts, and his soundlessness kept him in control.

Keys jingled at the lock on the loft door twenty feet across the room. Demyan didn't leave his spot or look away from the windows when the door opened. The darkness of the loft would do nothing to hide his silhouette sitting on the sill, though.

And he wanted Cavan to be afraid.

So terrified. Helpless like he made Ana. Without a choice or voice. Overpowered. Forced into pain and confusion.

The only difference between the two would come down to worth. Ana's was far more than Cavan Dolan's. Demyan would make damn sure the man knew it by the time he was done. Cavan would bleed, beg, and cry.

The door closed with a soft click. Demyan listened as feet shuffled and two thumps hit the wall. Shoes, likely. A light turned on, illuminating the apartment. Demyan still didn't turn from his position when he heard Cavan stumble and ask, "What the fuck?"

"I thought I made myself clear, Cavan," Demyan said coolly.

"How in the hell did you get in my—"

"Deadbolts on doors are useless when a fire escape leads straight to an unlocked window. Not that it would have made a difference, mind you. I was getting in, one way or the other."

Cavan sucked in a hard breath. "Get the fuck out, Demyan."

"No, see, I can't do that. Not after what you did to my sister."

"Oh, I think you can."

A gun clicked, the hammer drawing back. Demyan barked a bitter laugh, turning to stare straight at Cavan holding a handgun. "That's pointless."

"Really? Because right now, I'm the only one holding a

weapon worth using."

"Wrong," Koldan said, stepping out from the shadows of the small hallway. His own gun was cocked and loaded, pointing at Cavan with no shake. A silencer was attached to the end. "Toss it to the couch, now."

Cavan's gaze narrowed in Demyan's direction. "Couldn't do this alone?"

"I could, but I figured I owed him since he's looking out for her and all."

"Toss the goddamn gun," Koldan ordered.

Cavan's handgun flew to the couch cushion, forgotten.

"Don't bother jumping for any other weapons, either," Koldan added. "We cleared them out hours ago."

"You're not going to get away with this, Demyan. My family—"

"Means shit to me." Demyan swiveled his form around on the windowsill before dropping both feet to the floor. He stood, his stare never leaving Cavan. "In our world, we have a lot of rules. We stay in our own territories. We keep the peace between rival families. We do our business and stay out of others. But, most of all, we hand out respect. Not that any other girl you've attacked is worth any less than my sister, but Ana's got some clout behind her, Cavan. She's an Avdonin— a Bratva princess. You knew better. You knew this was coming."

"She wanted it," Cavan said, nearly smirking.

Anger flared in Demyan, but he beat back the urge to show it.

Cavan didn't relent. "Teased me for weeks like a good little whore, so what she got was exactly what she deserved after her show with your friend here."

Koldan took a step forward, his hand tightening around the butt of his handgun. "You cocksucking—"

"Don't," Demyan stated, flicking Koldan a look. "He's only running his mouth to shorten his time. The more he pisses me off, the quicker he thinks he's going to die. Isn't that right, Cavan?"

"Maybe, but that doesn't make what I said about your bitch of a sister any less true."

Demyan's jaw clenched, his teeth aching. "You know, I considered telling my father what you did to Ana so he could come along tonight. Anton Avdonin is pretty damn infamous in the business of killing. Liars have their tongues removed. Thieves lose their hands. Traitors get their bones crushed. I've witnessed men beg for someone else to do the deed when he walks into the room."

"Your point?" Cavan asked.

"I've never seen what he does to a rapist, let alone his daughter's. I think it would have been fascinating and terrifying all at once."

"Am I supposed to feel lucky it's you, then?"

This time, it was Demyan's turn to smirk. "Oh, no. See, I'm my father's son through and through. We bleed the same blood. He *made* me. I've picked up his tricks over the years. This will be far from easy for you, that I can guarantee."

"And you needed a lackey, why?" Cavan asked, tilting his head in Koldan's direction.

"He's just here for the show."

Demyan didn't blink when Cavan lurched forward to grab the gun he threw away earlier. A muffled pop filled the space before Cavan fell to the floor, holding his hand to his chest and shouting obscenities. Blood seeped from the new bullet wound he sported.

Koldan smiled. "Sorry, but not really."

"You bastard," Cavan hissed, rolling to his knees.

"Tell me the names you called my sister when you raped her," Demyan said, feeling almost emotionless.

"W-what?"

"I want to know the names you called my sister when you held her down and took what wasn't yours to have."

"I ..." Cavan blinked up at Demyan as he walked across the room slowly. He came to a stop only a foot away from Cavan's shaking form. "Why?"

Demyan's hand lifted, flashing the blade he held. "I'm

mighty fucking good with a knife. My hands don't shake. I never second-guess my cuts. A bit of blood isn't going to bother me. Your screams wouldn't, either. Don't worry, I'll make sure to slice your vocal cords so you won't bother anyone else in this building with your noise. For every name you called her, I'll carve a mark into your chest. When I'm done, I'll cut exactly what you are across your face so your family will know it, too—a rapist."

Finally, Demyan got what he wanted the most. Fear danced in Cavan's wide eyes.

"Does your uncle know what you do to girls, Cavan?" Demyan asked.

Cavan wouldn't answer.

"The names," Demyan said. "Give me them."

"I don't think—"

Demyan kicked out at Cavan, the toe of his boot catching the man under his jaw. Cavan's head snapped back with a sickening crack, blood spewing. Dark, cold chuckles echoed from Cavan's bleeding mouth.

"Whore," Cavan mumbled, shaking his head as he faced Demyan again. "Slut. Cunt. Bitch. Do you want more, Demyan? Do you want to know how she begged me to stop and how she bled for me, too? Worthless. Trash. Used."

Cavan sneered, the bloodiness of his mouth making the sight of him garish. "How about the way she bit her lip so hard when I kissed her, she bled into my mouth and it made me co—"

Fury rushed through Demyan like poison injected straight into his heart. He kicked Cavan again, harder the second time. It shut the fucker up instantly, but it also knocked him back to the floor, close to falling into unconsciousness.

Demyan couldn't have that. Quick as a blink, he leaned over, sliced his knife through the fabric of the guy's shirt, and cut straight across Cavan's sternum. The pain from the injury at an especially tender spot made Cavan's eyes fly wide and he shouted. A red ribbon of crimson pooled at the wound and fell to the floor.

Demyan was done playing games. He grabbed Cavan by the throat and squeezed. "I'll give you one chance to come at me, Cavan. Just the one. And then, I'm going to make you bleed my sister's justice to the ground. Try to make it worth it."

Cavan spat bloody saliva at Demyan but didn't move from the floor.

"I gave you your chance," Demyan said, unaffected. "Remember that."

Cavan struggled as Demyan grabbed him by the collar of his shirt and dragged him across the loft floor. Arms and feet thrashed to find purchase, but the man came up with nothing. Demyan came to a stop at the slight lift on the floor leading to the kitchen area. The useless strikes of Cavan's arms did nothing to deter Demyan from flipping the bastard onto his stomach and grabbing a fistful of his hair.

Demyan slammed his booted foot between Cavan's shoulder blades, pinning him in place as he yanked his head back roughly.

"Bite the ledge," Demyan ordered.

Cavan swallowed audibly. "Fuck you."

"Bite it, or I'll make you do it."

When Cavan still refused, Demyan nodded for Koldan to help. Koldan stayed silent while he forced a shouting Cavan's mouth to open against the edge of the ledge. Hard enough to do damage, but still keep the fucker lucid, Demyan's heel came down on the back of Cavan's head.

Blood, teeth, cartilage and fluid spilled to the floor in a mass of slop, followed by red vomit. Cavan choked as he retched and spat out blood. Demyan fisted Cavan's hair and pulled him up high enough for his knife to reach the correct spot at his throat to slice the vocal cords.

"I'm going to enjoy this, Cavan," Demyan whispered. "Scream for me."

Chapter Eight

Ana

"You seem better than last week," Viviana said.

Ana shrugged and picked at her *ptichie moloko*. The Russian dessert was one of her most favorite growing up and eating it always left her sentimental and missing her grandmamma Clarissa. "It's been ... okay, Ma."

"Good. I was worried about you, Ana. You can always come to me, you know? Or your father. He worries, too. So much."

Ana offered her mother a small smile. Then, she took a decent sized bite of the chocolate covered marshmallow sweet in an attempt to end the conversation. At least her side of it.

The week had gone by quietly, for the most part. Every day became a little easier to bear. Her anxiety wasn't necessarily lessened, but she didn't startle as badly as before. The dreams started to ebb. Food had its appeal again.

Mostly, her ease of mind came from Demyan. He promised it was over the morning after Koldan told her brother who her attacker really was. Ana didn't know why it was over, she didn't ask, and she sure as hell didn't plan to. But, inside, she knew it was. Well, the fear of Cavan was gone, anyway.

Koldan took her home to her apartment yesterday. Ana actually asked to go. She was ready to stand back up on her own two feet without Demyan's protection. Try to. She didn't expect it to be so hard walking back into her place, but it really, really was. Someone—she suspected her brother and Koldan—had cleaned the mess left over from her attack. It didn't help with the memories.

She stayed there. She slept that first night. Dreamed, too,

but slept.

Ana swallowed her sweet, noticing her mother watching her closely. "I'm good, Ma. Really."

Viviana nodded. "I know, baby. Does it maybe have something to do with a certain Russian hanging around your brother?"

Ana's grin formed before she could hide it. "You're nosy."

"Oh, yes. Very much. Even so, does it?"

"Has Daddy noticed, too?"

"Your father knows everything," Viviana said, winking. "Even when we think he doesn't."

Ana blew out a huff of air. Not everything. "How does he feel about it?"

"He's patiently waiting for Koldan to take him aside."

"We're not … together, or whatever. We hang out, talk and things. I like him. There's not much for him to discuss with Papa."

Viviana rapped her fingers to the countertop. "And that's why your father is patiently waiting and not knocking heads. Like I said, he knows, Ana."

Ah.

"Heads up, Erik!"

Ana didn't have time to react to a large male form bumping into her side. A football bounced off the stool beside hers. The liquor rack on the island took the brunt of both Erik and Ana's weight. It wasn't unusual for her father's close associates to be in their home. They were almost always sipping on vodka, sharing jokes that made Ana cringe, and sometimes they got a little rowdy.

Demyan loved football, Anton didn't. Ana overheard them arguing with Erik earlier about who could throw a better pass. That explained the ball and Erik.

It didn't explain the hard ball of panic swelling in her stomach as the glass liquor bottles shattered on the floor. The sounds of the shards tinkering and the liquid spilling across gray tiles sent her spinning right back into that night.

Ana couldn't breathe. She couldn't see anything but

darkness. The smell of her apartment floor was all around her. A memory of blood in her mouth made her taste buds sting. The decorative glass vase filled with gelled colors on her coffee table smashed to the floor.

Erik laughed deeply. Hands were on her body, righting her into the stool, but no one seemed to notice she was as stiff as a board, biting hard into her cheek, and fisting her hands into her stomach.

"Sorry, Ana girl." A very short beat of time passed before Erik said, "Ana? Ana, look at her me. It's okay, *milaya*. It's just me, Erik. Breathe, Ana."

"What's wrong?" Ana heard her mother whisper.

The trembling started in Ana's hands and quickly spread through the rest of her body like a raging forest fire. A heaviness settled on her chest with every short breath. She stumbled off the stool, hands flying out to keep anyone from coming closer.

The panic attack was relentless and damning.

In the background, she could hear her mother calling her name. Her father's worried words. Demyan's demands for everyone to give her space.

"I need you to count with me," Erik said faintly. "In, one, two, three, four, five and let it out, Ana. Again ..."

Someway, though she didn't have the first clue how he managed, Erik's voice caught her attention through the thick fog of terror. She followed his instructions over and over until the crushing waves lessened, her breathing became deeper and slower, and her vision cleared.

The shaking didn't relent as Erik watched her warily. "No more counting, just keep breathing."

Ana nodded, forcing herself to do as he said. She backed into the wall without realizing it. Like a dog being cornered. She couldn't bear to look around at the other faces in the room, so she focused only on Erik.

"How many fingers am I holding up?" Erik asked, waving a thumb and two fingers.

"Three," Ana said hoarsely.

"Good. Did you take your anxiety meds today?"

"She's not on any medications," Anton said from somewhere behind Erik.

He sounded so angry.

Ana broke into a fit of tears.

"Fuck, Anton, shut up," Erik growled. "Ana girl, look at me again. No meds?"

Ana shook her head, keeping her gaze on the ground.

"What triggered it? Was it me or the bottles breaking?"

"Bottles."

"What in the fuck is going on?" Anton demanded.

Ana glanced up just in time to see Erik toss her father a look over his shoulder. "You don't recognize it, do you?"

"Obviously not, Erik."

"Why didn't you tell me, Anton? I'm your friend. I wouldn't have said anything."

No, no, no, no, no.

Ana couldn't speak.

"Tell you what?"

"Look at her, man. This kind of an anxiety episode, it's induced by triggers from an attack."

"No," Anton breathed. "No, you're wrong."

"I am not. My first wife had them for years after her sexual assault before she committed suicide."

"Ana?" Viviana asked, crying softly.

Ana flinched away from her mother's call and the hands reaching toward her.

Anton, however, turned to his son. "Demyan?"

"She begged me not to tell you," Demyan confessed.

"Jesus Christ."

Ana wept harder. "I'm sorry."

• • •

"Why, Ana?" her father asked, his voice strained with emotion. "Why wouldn't you tell me?"

He kneeled down at her feet. Ana stayed stock still

perched on the couch, fighting off the urge to cry or run. Viviana sat beside her daughter, hand holding tight to Ana's while tears rolled down her cheeks soundlessly. When Anton asked Ana to recount the attack, she did so in monotone with her gaze stuck to the wall where the clock was ticking down.

Everyone was silent. No one moved. They kept watching.

"Why?" Anton asked again, the word full of air.

"I didn't want you to blame me," she whispered. "I thought … I thought I did something wrong and you would be disappointed."

"For fuck's sake, Ana, I would never—" Anton clamped his mouth shut, tipping his head down to meet his palm.

"And I was scared," Ana continued. "Of him and what might happen if I said anything."

Anton frowned. "How long ago?"

"Two weeks," Demyan said quietly where he was leaning against the wall.

"You shut up," Anton growled, glaring. "Her I can understand, but you, Demyan. *You …*"

"Please don't be angry with him," Ana said, sniffling. "He only did what I asked."

"He knows better." Anton didn't relent in his harsh, angry stare. "He knows what I can—"

"Same thing I did," Demyan interrupted their father sharply.

Anton sighed, his tongue peeking out to wet his lips as he regarded Ana again. "Cavan Dolan?"

"Yes."

"I thought you warned him off, Demyan?"

"Me, too."

Anton cleared his throat, never looking away from Ana. "The body found last Wednesday in the loft uptown. They weren't releasing names at the time. That's on you, yes?"

"Yeah," Demyan answered.

"Ana," her father drawled softly, his hands coming to rest on her wrists. "Tell me what you need."

"Please don't blame me," Ana said.

Anton's gaze met his wife's, something unspoken passing between them. "I don't know what's worse, Ana. That you felt you couldn't come to me, or that you feel like I might say it was your fault. They both hurt me just the same. What did I do to make you so distrustful and doubting of me? I love you."

Ana's heart hurt. "I know, Papa."

"You've always been my little girl. You always come to me when you need something."

"And that's exactly why, isn't it, Ana?" her mother asked. "Because he sees you as his princess, and treats you like it, too. You didn't want him to think you were tainted or ruined. How would he look at you after, knowing? Am I right?"

Ana cringed, refusing to answer.

"I'd say so, Vine," Anton murmured. "I'm so sorry. So, so sorry, Ana. I will always love you, no matter what. You're mine. If I've ever made you feel anything less, I'm sorry. And it's not your fault, my *dushka*."

More than anything, Ana needed to hear those words from her father the most.

• • •

Ana woke to yells coming from down the hall. She sat up on the bed and looked around her old room, confused. After the shit show earlier, all she wanted to do was sleep. Her parents hadn't pushed her for anything more than she gave them, so they let her go to bed without an argument.

Standing from the bed, she padded out of her room and down the hall. The shouts became clearer the closer she came to father's office.

"What would you have done, then?" Demyan asked, sounding derisive and angry.

"I'd—"

"Murdered him," her brother interrupted their father. "You would have slaughtered him, Papa. Painted the fucking city with his blood and then bathed in it. I know you ... I

77

fucking *am* you, okay."

"Demyan, calm down," Viviana said quietly.

Ana came to a stop just outside the office door. She stayed hidden in the darkness of the hallway where no one inside would be able to see her, but she also couldn't see them.

"What are we going to do, now?" Anton barked. "They've got a small syndicate in the city worth nothing compared to us, but the family in Detroit is *massive*. If he sends men down here, it will be the biggest war New York has seen in a century."

"I know," Demyan said. "But I made a choice. I don't regret it."

"What about Freddie?"

Demyan made an uncomfortable sound. "There's a problem with that."

"Oh?"

"Yeah, he's missing. Has been since the day after they found the body."

"Shit," Anton hissed.

"What does that mean?" Viviana asked.

"It means Freddie was likely one of the few people Cavan had contact with outside of his family," Anton explained. "Demyan got his info from Freddie. It'll lead right back to us. There's no keeping it quiet."

"But ... he raped her, Anton."

"I know, baby. I fucking know what he did to her."

"They're not like the Italians, Ma," Demyan said. "They don't follow rules like Cosa Nostra. The family is involved heavily in human-trafficking, so they have little regard for human life as it is. I did some checking on Cavan and his time back in Detroit. Ana is not the first girl. There are others, but they've been quieted with money, the stories have all but disappeared, and it was like it never even happened."

"My God."

"He got what he deserved," Demyan added.

"I'm not disagreeing with you," Anton said, sighing heavily. "But this is going to be a mess—a bad one."

"I'm not sorry."

"Go home, Demyan," Viviana murmured. "Go home to Gia."

"I should," her brother agreed.

Ana took a few steps backward before Demyan came into the hall. He didn't say a thing when he noticed her eavesdropping.

Ana couldn't meet Demyan's stare. "I'm sorry he's mad at you."

"Come here, *sestra*," Demyan said, pulling Ana into a tight hug. "Don't worry about his anger with me. Papa will get over it, eventually. Everything I did was worth it, especially for you."

"Okay."

Demyan kissed the top of Ana's head before releasing her. "I need to get home to Gia. Are you fine here?"

Ana nodded. "Yeah. Thanks, Demyan."

"There's nothing to thank me for."

Ana thought there was because she was only now learning how much her brother really did care for and loved her. "You're going to be a great father."

Demyan grinned. "I hope so."

Ana waited for her brother to disappear down the stairs before she went back to the office doorway.

The sounds of several items crashing to the floor stopped her from knocking. Her father stood over his desk, his fists pressed into the top as his shoulders heaved with silent sobs. Pain creased lines over his face while his teeth were bared and clenched tight. Everything from the desk lamp, from his laptop, knickknacks, and even his treasured photos were a broken pile on the floor. Her mother stood behind him, stoic and quiet.

"It'll be okay, Anton."

"Will it, really?" he asked, tremors rocking his hands. "You don't know Liam Dolan, Vine."

"We'll figure something out."

Anton growled in anguish. "I'm so sick, baby. In my

fucking heart, it hurts. What he did to her—how do I get her to forgive me for not protecting her like I was supposed to?"

"You're not Superman."

"I was supposed to be hers."

Chapter Nine

Demyan

"*Mmmm.*" Gia hummed, swallowing the last bit of chocolate covered fruit. She rested back into the half a dozen plush pillows on the king-sized bed. "Best surprise ever."

Demyan grinned from the recliner. "You deserve it, babe."

Gia pursed her lips, teasingly. "Do I?"

"Sure. You work so hard with the kids, you're seven and a half months pregnant and tired most days. Worst of all, you put up with my sorry ass."

Her laughter rung out in the hotel room. It was five-star all the way. Gourmet food. A million dollar view. Anything and everything Gia could want was just a phone call away. Demyan hadn't told her yet, but there was more to this last minute getaway then she really knew.

Liam Dolan was flying into the city on Sunday morning and a meeting had been set up for Monday afternoon. Anton believed the best way to get ahead of the game was to hit first before they could try to strike you. So, instead of waiting for someone to come to them about Cavan's death, Demyan's father sent someone to them.

Hence, the early December meeting.

If there was anything Demyan's father taught him that was more important than the rest, it was getting your loved ones to a safe place when shit was about to go down. Demyan would have preferred to take Gia out of state altogether, but he didn't think that would go over too well with her. His mother and sister were two floors down with his father, but Gia wasn't aware of that yet, either.

"Hey, where did you go over there?" Gia asked.

Demyan shook his thoughts away, not wanting to give her any inclination of his worries. "Nowhere, babe. I'm here with you, like always."

Gia waved at the large, beautiful hotel room. "We have this place for the rest of the weekend, huh?"

"A little longer," Demyan said. "Maybe the week, too."

"Demyan, I have work on Monday."

"Second surprise, I called in your emergency vacation time."

"Demyan!"

He gave her a look that pinned her back into the bed. "Listen, after everything that's happened over the last little while, we both needed a break. You're almost done work, anyway."

"Exactly," Gia said quietly. "And I really wanted to spend as much time with the kids as I could before I finished."

Guilt ate at Demyan's insides. He hated lying to Gia, but she was too goddamn fearless for her own good. If he told her the truth about why she was there, she was liable to tell him to fuck off and away she would go. "I'm sorry. I thought this would be nice for us before the baby came, that's all. Like a last hurrah."

Gia sighed, side-eyeing him. Then, her pretty pink lips curved into a sly grin. One that spoke of sin, sex, and heaven all rolled into one. Demyan knew that look on her well. His cock hardened at the sight alone.

Gia crooked a finger in his direction. "Come here."

"Hmm, you sure?"

"So sure. You, right here," Gia said, pointing to herself. "Now."

Demyan didn't need to be told a second time. He tugged off his shirt as he crossed the room before unbuckling his slacks and kicking off the pants. His knees hit the bottom of the bed and he crawled up the sheets watching her like prey.

Gia had already situated herself on the bed in nothing but one of his T-shirts and lace panties earlier, so by the time he fitted himself between the sweetness of her thighs, she had her top gone, too.

Under Demyan's palms, Gia's skin was warm silk and

crushed velvet. She shivered beneath his hands kneading the soft flesh of her ass. Grinding her lace covered core to his groin, she moaned into the kiss he crushed to her lips. She was soaking through her panties already and Demyan couldn't wait to feel her hot and wet around his dick.

"Love you, *katyonak*. God, how I love you."

Gia grinned, her tongue flicking out to tease along the seam of his mouth. "Forever?"

"Always, babe."

"Good. You and me against the world, right?"

"Damn right."

By Gia's demand, he made quick work of removing what little clothes they still wore. Her fingers interweaved with his on the pillow above her head as he slid home inside her sex with a groan that rocked him from the inside out. Gia's head tipped back to the pillow as her thighs widened to take him deeper.

Her pussy was a slick paradise. Pure ecstasy encompassing him. It drove him to the brink of in-fucking-sanity every single time he loved her.

"Christ, yeah," Demyan said in an exhale. "Perfect. You're so perfect."

Gia's teeth caught her bottom lip, her blue eyes darkening as she watched him above her. Demyan kept their rhythm slow, wanting to draw it out as long as possible. Gia was his queen, she always had been, and she deserved to be worshiped like one.

The pregnancy made Gia sensitive in ways Demyan loved. It didn't take a whole hell of a lot to get her going and she climbed high and fast before dropping just as hard from her peaks. She was downright insatiable and he adored giving her all she wanted of him.

Every thrust of his body was met with the rise of her hips. His mouth explored the creamy skin of her chest and up to her collarbones. He licked, kissed and sucked on her neck to the line of her jaw. Demyan felt her walls begin to contract with a rushing orgasm. Gia came undone around him, shaking with his name in her beautiful mouth. Releasing one of her hands, he wrapped his arm around her back and rolled them over so she was on top.

Gia lifted his hand still connected with hers and kissed the tattoo on the skin between his forefinger and thumb. A small, black cross. Simple and brand new to his body. It was the first time she openly gave it any attention since he had it done two days earlier.

Demyan had always refused the Bratva tradition of tattoos. Ink wasn't his style, and despite his father's very vocal arguments about the meaning of the designs, he still never had one done.

Until Cavan's death.

The single cross marked a worthy hit in the Bratva.

Gia undoubtedly knew why it was there though she didn't say a thing.

She rocked on top of him, his hands keeping her supported. Her blonde curls fell over her shoulders, covering her breasts. "Why are we really here, Demyan?"

His gaze snapped to hers. "I told you, babe."

"Please don't lie to me. I know there's a lot going on you're not telling me about."

Demyan licked his lips, trying to focus on her and not the urge to come curling in his lower half. "There's a meeting on Monday. It's safer if you're out of sight."

"Okay," Gia said, her brilliant, sexy smile back in a blink. She squeezed her inner muscles around his shaft, taking his air away and sending pleasure rocketing through his bloodstream. "Never lie to me, Demyan."

Demyan let his head fall back into the pillows with a moan. "Shit, don't stop doing that."

"Oh, you know I won't."

• • •

Liam Dolan was an icy man. Not just icy, no, deathly fucking cold.

Demyan didn't think he had ever sat face to face with someone as entirely emotionless as the human being sitting across from him now. Liam even spoke with no sentiment or care. The man didn't seem to get angry, he barely blinked, and his stare was practically dead.

It was … disturbing.

Liam snapped his fingers once in the air when his plate was empty. A man stepped in to remove the item, utensils, and napkin. He was arrogant enough that he refused to allow the restaurant's servers to attend him.

"Anything else, Boss?"

"Rum and coke," Liam stated, never looking away from Demyan. "Very little coke."

"May we speak now, Liam?" Anton asked, leaning back in his chair beside Demyan. "I've let you have your meal, let your men search any of us they wanted, and whatever else you demanded. I think it's time to discuss what happened."

Liam shrugged. "If you desire it, but I think we both know how the conversation will end, Anton."

Demyan didn't, but those words put him on edge instantly.

Only a few of his father's men were inside the restaurant, but the outside was swarmed with Bratva. In cars, behind the business, sitting out front on the benches, and even in the businesses surrounding the place.

Anton took no chances.

"I don't believe I do know how it will end," Anton said, raising a brow.

"Truthfully, I have very little interest in talking to you."

Anton canted his head, eyes narrowing. "In Brighton Beach, I am the boss, Liam. I speak for my men here. They don't speak for even themselves when I'm around."

Liam nodded, his expression stony. "I can respect that, but I asked you to let me speak on a straightforward, no bullshit basis with the young man who killed my nephew."

"And that young man is my son, so again—"

"It won't really matter, you know," Liam interjected,

sounding bored. "We can argue all day, but I will still get what I came for all the same, Russian."

Demyan practically heard his father's teeth crack beneath his clenching jaw.

"He raped my sister," Demyan said, wanting to get the dinner over with. The longer he sat in Liam Dolan's company, the closer to death he felt. "He brutally attacked, threatened, and left her bruised and bleeding on her apartment floor. If it was your daughter—"

"I have no daughter, so your point is moot."

Stunned at the man's lack of empathy, Demyan didn't quite know what to say.

"If you wish to appeal to some sympathetic part of me, I can promise it will be useless and you will fail, Demyan Avdonin. I have nothing to feel compassion for. No wife, very little family worth my time or breath, and nothing I have is something I would fight to keep from losing. Especially now that you've taken my nephew from me."

"He raped my daughter," Anton snapped. "And she was not the first girl he attacked, Liam."

Liam turned to take the rum and coke from his man. Slowly, he sipped from the drink while he watched Demyan in that unnerving way of his. Demyan could smell how strong the rum in the drink was from across the table, but Liam continued downing it as if it were water. Liam didn't react at all to Anton's statement and he also didn't seem to notice how thick the tension in the room was around him.

Who the fuck was this man?

The tumbler glass dangled from the tips of Liam's fingers uncaringly. "I've always believed women are only good for a few things. None of them are worth killing for, mind you, but they're always worth taking."

"Let's agree to disagree on that opinion," Demyan muttered, nausea pounding at his insides.

"We're all entitled to them. Women can easily become even the coldest man's weakness. It's Gia, right?" Liam asked.

Demyan stilled, feeling every eye at the table turn on him

and Liam. "She has nothing to do with this."

"Oh, but she has everything to do with you, my boy."

Steely, green eyes surveyed Demyan from across the table. A shiver ran up his spine as Liam tossed back the remainder of his rum and coke. Liam picked up his vibrating cell phone from the table, glanced at the screen, sighed, and set it back down without a word. It was as if he had been waiting for that message, whatever it was.

Dread filled Demyan to the brim.

"I was going to do to her what you did to my nephew," Liam said drily. "It would have been nothing less than what you deserved for his suffering."

Demyan's heart beat wildly. "His suffering was earned."

Liam smiled grimly. "Perhaps, but it was still going to earn her the same fate, nonetheless. Then I learned of her condition. Seven and a half months pregnant. A little girl, they told me."

Not his baby. Not his daughter.

Demyan's mind fell silent.

No one moved around him. No one else spoke.

Demyan's hands curled around the edge of the table, his fingernails breaking against the wood from the pressure. Something inside was screaming for him to leave, but his feet felt like cement stuck to the floor.

"I couldn't help but consider the child, you see." Liam ghosted the tip of his index finger around the rim of the glass. "I'm a monster, but unborn babies … I don't know how that might affect me. Would the baby suffer pain like her mother? They're attached while she's safe and comfortable in her warm home. Would she feel the skin being cut from the bone and the life leaving? Would it hurt?"

Bile rose in Demyan's throat.

"Just as well, I suppose," Liam murmured. "You might not see her mutilated, you won't wonder how long she lived, or even if she begged for her life, but you will lose two. I believe that'll settle our scores. They'll make it quick, Demyan. For the child's sake. It was my only request of them and my olive branch to you."

"*No.*"

Demyan stood so fast his chair toppled out from beneath him. Spinning on his heel, he headed toward the front door of the restaurant before anyone would say a thing otherwise.

Gia was safe, he reminded himself. She was in hiding like he left her that morning. No one knew where she was. They couldn't touch her. No harm would come to her or his baby. Liam seemed so sure that Demyan couldn't shake the awful feeling gnawing at his gut.

Demyan fumbled with his cell phone, his shoulders trembling and his back aching. He had to stop walking just so he was able to hold the phone steady and dial Gia's number.

"Your nephew was a fucking sociopath," Anton growled from somewhere behind Demyan. "You knew what he was, hid his transgressions, paid off his victims, and sent him away to hurt someone else. How dare you say the life of an unborn child—my grandchild—is worth the same as his?"

"Because, when blood is spilled, more must fall to answer for it," Liam replied softly.

"Then why not me?" Anton asked, his shout filling the restaurant with his pain. "*Me,* Liam. He's my son. I would have answered for it."

The phone call rang and rang. Demyan pressed it harder to his ear, keeping his swaying body steady by leaning against the wall.

Pick up, Gia. Pick up.

"We all learn, eventually. Apparently, it's Demyan's time to be taught. Taking your life would have done little for my lesson if there's only one person he loves with his entire being, after all."

"This is not over," Anton whispered viciously. "The score is not settled. I will ruin you, Liam. I don't care if takes me thirty years."

"I welcome your efforts, Anton."

"Hello?"

Relief flowed from Demyan in a whoosh of air. "Gia,

hey."

"Hey. Everything going okay?" his sweet girl asked.

Demyan swallowed the rising lump clogging his throat. "Yeah. You're still at the hotel, right?"

A beat of silence answered his question.

"Gia, please tell me you're still at the hotel, babe," Demyan managed to say though he didn't know how.

"I got a call from the school about the substitute. You didn't give me a chance to plan for this, Demyan, and the schedule for the next week is at home, so I grabbed a cab—"

"No." Demyan pushed off the wall and slammed the restaurant door open, walking out into the blinding light and cold December air. "Gia, *no*."

"What's wrong?"

"Where are you right now?"

"Just unlocking the front door. I'll be in and out quick, I promise. It wasn't like I was driving one of our cars. I grabbed the sweater you left with the hoodie to keep my face hidden. Nobody would know it was me. It'll be fine."

None of those things mattered, Demyan knew. Chances were, Liam had men waiting for her at all their homes. Demyan's heart fell from his chest to the ground. He could literally feel every piece of it break and shatter while his soul crumbled.

Demyan didn't want to frighten her by telling her. He didn't want her to feel as though it was her fault. It wasn't. He did this.

It might be easier if she never had to see it coming.

"I love you, Gia," Demyan said softly. "I love you so, so much, babe."

"I know. I love you, too."

Demyan walked down the street, ignoring the people passing him along the way. He stared at the cloudless sky, thinking of earlier times. "Remember when I said I would always follow you?"

Gia laughed. The tinkling sound wrapped and suffocated Demyan in her love and life. Just like it always had. "Yeah, we were so young."

"You had that yellow dress on."

"My favorite one."

Demyan chuckled. "And you were so pissed off because you stained it with mud."

"Funny, we knew even then how we were going to end up. Would you still follow me, Demyan?"

"I always will, Gia."

Streaks of wetness made roads down his cheeks. Demyan came to a stop beside his vehicle.

"Find what you needed?" Demyan asked.

"Yeah, it was—" Gia cut off with a sharp gasp.

His heart broke further.

"I love you," he told her. Just so she would know and those could be the last words she heard. When the gunshot popped on the other end of the call, Demyan said it one more time. "I love you, Gia."

Chapter Ten

Ana

Resting on the couch with her mother's arm wrapped protectively around her, Ana felt like a little girl all over again. Viviana's fingers stroked soothingly through Ana's dark hair as they watched a chick flick.

"This reminds me of when you were younger," Viviana said.

Ana leaned back and grinned at her mother. "I was just thinking that. Demyan says I was a brat, though."

"You were difficult as a child—spoiled, demanding, and you had way too much attitude for your own good. Don't get me wrong, you've turned into someone amazing, but back then I wondered if you ever would. You got all that defiance from your father, too. I swear Anton encouraged you to be this little hellcat from the moment you were born.

"Like he wanted you to break balls and take names later. *If she doesn't want to share, she doesn't have to share, Vine, it's her shit and nobody needs to take it from her*, he'd say. He might as well have been shouting at the universe to let you have your cake because you were his daughter and he said so."

Ana laughed. "Really?"

"Yeah, and he's so proud of you, Ana. I get to be his moon, stars, and sun, but you kids are his world. The thing keeping him living and breathing."

"I know."

"Little kids, little problems; big kids, big problems," Viviana said, sighing.

"What's that?"

"An old proverb. No parent really understands it until their babies aren't babies anymore and something bad comes along that we can't protect you from. I think that's the hardest part about watching you and Demyan grow up. The bigger you got, the less we could help. It's like we had to shove you both into the world and hope for the best."

Ana glanced down at her fidgeting hands, remembering her father's words to her mother a few nights ago in his office. "Do you feel like you failed me, Ma?"

"I don't know how to feel anything else, Ana. We've always been so careful about knowing who we were letting into our home. We had to be and he went right by us. So yeah, we failed and I'm sorry."

"Someday, we have to walk on our own, too. You can't be responsible for things out of our control."

Viviana blew out a huff of air. "The day that happens will be when they put me six feet underground, Ana. It might feel like you're walking alone sometimes, but all you have to do is look behind you. We're not too far away, we're just letting you learn the ropes."

Ana was never more grateful for her mother than she was now. Viviana was the kind of woman Ana wanted to be. Quietly strong, relentless, and loving.

"Adrik called your father yesterday to chat."

Ana stilled at her mother's admission. "Why is Koldan's father calling Papa?"

"Well, they talk a lot, you know. About things on the business side of life."

"That doesn't answer my question."

"No, I suppose it doesn't. He wanted to know if he should ask Koldan to come back to Jersey for a while. He thought maybe you would need some breathing room after everything. I guess Koldan downright refuses to leave unless you ask him to."

Ana blinked, surprised. Her words lodged in her throat as she sat up from her mother's embrace and turned on the couch so her feet were on the floor. "How does Adrik know?"

Had Koldan told him?

"With the meeting happening today, there were a lot of

questions asked about why. Things like what Demyan did can't happen just because he wants to. There has to be a reason. Your father explained to a few people the circumstance."

"And word traveled fast," Ana finished for her mother.

"Yes, I'm sorry."

"Everybody will know."

It was exactly what she didn't want.

"No one will think it's your fault, Ana."

"But they're still going to know, Ma. Every time someone looks at me, they won't see me. They'll see what he did to me."

"No, they'll see you're still breathing," Viviana said sharply. "They'll see you're walking, smiling, and alive. Strength, that's what they'll see."

"Oh."

The cell phone on the table rang a familiar tune. The one Ana knew her mother had designated to her father's number. Instantly, Viviana's gaze snapped to the clock on the hotel room's wall.

"It's too early," she said faintly. "He shouldn't be calling now."

Viviana sat upright, snatching the ringing device up and answering the call. "Anton?"

Ana watched in frightened silence as her mother's face fell, tears glistened, and pain followed every breath.

"Which hospital?" Viviana asked. "Yeah, we're coming. Get him calm, even if they have to sedate him to do it."

The phone was placed back to the table, forgotten. Viviana stared out the large window overlooking the city. They were right in the heart of it. Somewhere her father said they would be safest, or as close as they could be with all the people and cameras watching. Who would try to hurt them here?

"Ma?" Ana asked.

Viviana made an indescribable noise. "Gia was shot."

Ana's heart stopped. "No, she's two floors up, Ma."

"I guess she left. She was at their apartment ..." Viviana stood, turning fast to grab her purse and coat from the recliner. "Come on, we have to get to the hospital."

"Is she okay?"

"Come on, Ana, hurry."

Ana grabbed her mother's wrist and yanked, stopping her. She needed to know. There were so many things running wild in her mind. Her brother. How much she adored his fiancée. Gia was pregnant, too. With her niece. Far enough along for the baby to survive if born now, but still. What if?

"Ma, is she okay?"

"A neighbor heard the shot, found her, and performed CPR while they called nine-one-one. Ivan was notified when they got Gia to the hospital. They're having a difficult time calming Demyan down and he's causing issues at the hospital. We have to go, Ana. That's all I know. I have to be with Demyan."

Ana gathered her own things, sending out a quick message to Koldan before she pulled on her shoes. As they were leaving the hotel, she asked her mother, "Where was she shot?"

Viviana struggled for words before blurting, "In the side of the head."

• • •

Ana swayed on her feet, turning a wide circle in the Emergency waiting room. She didn't know where her mother had gone. They wouldn't allow Ana to go back through the doors to find her family. The only reason Viviana was allowed through was for the sake of her son.

No one would tell Ana anything about Gia, her brother or the state of her unborn niece. Some nurses gave her a pitiful, remorseful smile when she asked—demanded—answers, but it got her nowhere. She was pretty sure she caught a glimpse of her father and Ivan when Gia's sisters pushed through the entrance doors an hour earlier, but who knew, really.

This was chaos.

Loud voices getting louder. Constant movement.

People were watching her, but she didn't know who they were. Some faces she had met before, some were friends of her mother's and father's, but most she couldn't place. None made any attempt to talk to her.

Ana knew she was crying, but numbness settled in deep. It burrowed throughout, turning everything slow and holding her panic at bay.

"Ana!"

Through the crowd of people, one finally stood out. Koldan's embrace came swift and hard, swallowing her whole and making her disappear from the room for just a brief moment. But it was long enough. She shook and cried, burying her face in his unzipped leather jacket, fisting her hands into his shirt, and her knees buckled. Koldan didn't let her fall. His arm wrapped her lower back, holding her close to his form while his other hand tangled in her hair.

"Hey, calm down," he whispered.

"They won't tell me anything!"

"They probably don't know, or can't tell you, Ana."

"But the baby is my niece, so that makes me family, right?"

"I don't know how hospital policy works and as far as I know, Gia's in surgery."

Ana's hands clenched harder. "But—"

"The very best neurosurgeons in the city work here, Ana. This was the best place to bring someone with severe brain trauma. It'll be okay."

All the worry and anguish suddenly came out like a tidal wave intent on destroying what bit of composure she had left. Koldan held strong and waited her through it. When she finally felt calm enough to think clearly, anger burst through her sadness.

"Where were you?" Ana demanded, smacking him in the chest. "I called you two hours ago!"

Koldan snagged her hand in his to keep her from hitting

him again. "Stop it, Ana. I was there."

Ana froze. "With Gia?"

"No, at the sit-down. I was outside in a car. When Demyan came outside, he looked blitzed, so I followed him down the street. I had to take his phone from him, but I listened before I hung it up. I could hear the person trying to help Gia." Koldan grimaced, blowing out a shaky breath of air. "I had a job to do. I was in the group that needed to make sure Liam and his fools departed the city like they were supposed to after the meeting."

"Oh."

"Yeah, but I'm sorry I couldn't come right away."

Ana nodded, feeling awful for being contrite. "Did they leave?"

"They caught a private jet thirty minutes ago," he confirmed.

"Was the meeting bad?"

Koldan shrugged. "I'm not sure, *krasivyy*. I wasn't inside the restaurant, but I know the aftermath was … insane. I guess Liam made the decision on Gia because of what Demyan did. There wasn't much time to talk. Everyone wanted to get out of there as fast as possible, especially once Ivan got the call from the hospital."

Ana glanced around, sensing people looking at her and Koldan. Sure enough, people were staring. "Who are these men?"

"Bratva," Koldan answered.

"My father's?"

"Yeah."

"Why do they keep looking at us like we're a fucking circus show?"

"Because, I'm the son of Adrik Vasin," Koldan said, barely audible.

"And I'm the daughter of Anton Avdonin."

"You got it, Ana."

Well, then.

Ana refused to pay the gawkers any more attention.

"Ma said Gia was shot in the head," Ana said, feeling distant.

"I heard."

"How do you survive a gunshot to the head, Koldan?"

"I ..."

He couldn't finish the sentence.

Ana didn't need him to.

• • •

"Wake up, *krasivyy*. Time for some news."

The soothing, dark tenor of Koldan wrapped Ana in security. Ana blinked awake, an ache in her back throbbing as she sat up straight in the uncomfortable hospital chair. She wiped the sleep from her eyes, trying to get some focus into her brain. Where was she again? The antiseptic smell and quiet shuffle of feet reminded her.

The hospital. Gia. The baby.

Oh, God.

"Ana?"

Her mother's voice woke Ana up completely. She shook the rest of her sleepiness off, but the heavy emotions still weighed her down. "Hey, Ma."

Viviana tried to smile as she sat down beside Ana. Tried being the key word, because it looked anything but true. "I'm sorry I couldn't come find you earlier. They're not going to let anyone in the room with Gia until morning and no one can be in the NICU except for immediate family to the child. Apparently, they don't consider an aunt immediate family. They're letting your father and me in, though."

The NICU?

The NICU.

"The baby is okay?" Ana asked

"It was touch and go for a while," Viviana replied. "She was in distress so they made the choice to take her. She's beautiful. A little small. Looks just like Gia with Demyan's dark hair."

"What about Gia?"

Viviana looked down at her hands. Ana followed the stare to see tremors were rocking her mother's fists. Only then did Ana notice her mother's eyes were red-rimmed and puffy. Like she spent the whole day crying. "The neighbor who called nine-one-one, they did the best they could until the ambulance arrived. Gia had a heartbeat, but it was weak and her breathing was very shallow. She was unresponsive and getting worse. She didn't make it to the hospital before they lost her heartbeat."

"But, they brought her back, right?"

"For a short while," Viviana murmured. "They lost it once more in surgery, and then brought it back again."

"What aren't you telling me, Ma?"

"Gia's in a coma, Ana. She's still unresponsive. They said she lost her brain function in surgery. There's no activity on the monitors. Right now, she's on life support. It's breathing for her and making her heart pump blood like it needs to. But when they take her off ..."

Ana felt Koldan's arm find her waist, holding tight.

"... She won't breathe and her heart won't beat," Viviana finished.

Chapter Eleven

Demyan

She was sleeping. Demyan's tiny two kilogram daughter rested inside an incubator. She was dark-haired, like him. No doubt blue-eyed, too, but he couldn't be sure until she woke up and opened her eyes. The tiny creature looked like Gia. The way her nose curved to the tip, the pout of her pink lips, and the height of her cheekbones.

Just like her mother but for the black lashes fanning her pale skin.

Skin the doctor explained had been blue when they finally pulled her from Gia's body.

Small, heart-shaped bandages held the oxygen tubes secure to her puffy cheeks. A feeding tube had been inserted through her right nostril. Leads for monitors were placed on her chest and stomach, recording her respiratory actions and heartrate. She was naked but for a diaper and yellow hat that seemed to swallow her little body whole.

Demyan didn't know what to do.

"She's a little tiny but seems mostly healthy," his mother said softly. "They're concerned about the oxygen loss. They'll do more tests over the next couple of weeks and whatever results you get should give you some kind of outlook on what to expect. There's the long term to consider, but you won't be able to know how this will have affected her until she's a bit older. Say like when she should be reaching normal milestones."

He was hearing his mother, but the words weren't adding up.

"Uh ..." Demyan cleared his dry throat. "I don't understand."

"Brain damage," Anton clarified. "It's a possibility. A

small one, but it is there. Demyan—"

"Brain damage?" he asked hoarsely. "My baby might have brain damage?"

It was something Demyan hadn't considered.

"Ana went without oxygen for several minutes. Close to the same amount of time. She was fine," his father rushed to say. "Don't jump to conclusions just yet."

Demyan nodded, but on the inside, everything was recoiling with fear and panic.

The NICU had wide open windows as a way to allow a safe method for family and friends to visit the babies. Familiar faces of men Demyan had grown up surrounded by stared in through the glass. Bratva men who were there for his father, Ivan, and himself. His heart was breaking, his world was shattering and he couldn't keep control.

"Papa," he started to say, something awful swirling in his stomach as he stared at the men looking back.

"Close the curtains," Anton demanded.

"Anton—"

"Close the damn curtains, Vine!" he shouted. "Now!"

Demyan's mother shut out the outside world just in time. The sickness rising in his stomach spilled into a garbage can as the tears fell. Demyan's knees hit the hard floor with a crack as he grappled for purchase on the rim of the can. Dry heaves were followed by his sobs. Cries violent enough to shake his entire frame. The bile burned on the back of his tongue. A dizzying sensation had him swaying on the spot. The edges of his vision darkened.

"He's sick, so he needs to leave. He can't be in here with an immune-compromised infant," Demyan heard a nurse say in a way that had his anger boiling. "Even if it is his daughter."

"He isn't sick," Viviana snapped. "He's in *pain*. His fiancée is on life support and his newborn daughter is in the NICU."

"Vine—"

"No, Anton. She should know better. I don't give a fuck who you are, because I sure as shit know who *we* are. You might not know us right now, but trust that you will before the day is done. You need to leave," Viviana demanded.

"Excuse me? You can't order me—"

"Get out and send in a new nurse or so help me God, lady, you won't have a damned job to come to tomorrow!"

Demyan felt the strong arm of his father wrap around his chest. Anton held tight, rocking his son in a side-to-side motion gently. More tears fell. His teeth clenched so hard beneath his tightened jaw that they literally fucking ached. Just like his heart and soul.

"Please don't tell me it's going to be okay," Demyan managed to say. The trembling in his hands covered the rest of his body. "Please."

"I won't, son. I won't do anything you don't want me to."

Demyan wasn't sure how long he stayed like that. Immobile and stricken by his grief and shock. Apparently long enough for an older nurse to take the previous position of the one his mother kicked out. Anton finally let his son go to stand. Demyan glanced up at the woman when she placed her hand on his clenched fist. Her soft stare and tender smile remind him of Sasha, his grandmother who had died a few months after his twenty-third birthday.

"Hi. My name is Jeannie," the woman said, speaking in a hushed tone. "I'm going to be taking care of your new baby girl for the rest of the shift. Does she have a name?"

Demyan nodded. Yes, she had a name. "Vera. Gia wanted to call her Vera."

"Okay. That's a great name. Have you held her? We can get you cleaned up and we'll be careful with the tubes and wires. If you want to sit and rock her, we can do that, too."

A passing look at the sleeping baby in the incubator sent Demyan's panic spinning out of control again. She was too tiny for him to hold. He would probably break her. "I can't."

"Of course you can, Demyan," his father said. "She's your daughter."

"No, she's so little. I don't want to hurt her."

"I understand your concern. Don't be worried about her

size," the nurse said. "It's extremely important for her to have skin-to-skin contact with someone, especially one of her parents. Right now, it'll be even more beneficial for her to have it. She's been out in the world for how long?"

Demyan blinked, unsure. "A few hours, maybe."

Anton coughed. "About twelve, actually."

Had that much time passed already?

Jeannie smiled sadly. "And she's not felt her mother or father once. The world is not the same as where she spent the last few months growing and thriving. It's much more frightening without some kind of familiar comfort. She's heard your voice before. She'll know who you are. The way you smell, how you sound, and the way your touch feels. It's the best kind of love for a baby. She needs to feel you, okay. Please."

Demyan couldn't argue with that. He wasn't allowed to see Gia, yet, for whatever reason. He could do this for Vera. "I can't hold her. Not yet."

"You don't have to hold her to touch her. Let's wash your hands and arms first."

Under the nurse's supervision and instruction, Demyan scrubbed his skin until it felt raw. The older lady spoke to his parents all the while, discussing Vera's condition and the circumstances of her traumatic birth. Demyan almost felt as if he was watching the scene from above and not actually in the moment like he truly was.

Demyan waited as the nurse opened up the two portholes on the side of the incubator. She waved him over and explained that even just his hands on the baby's skin could and would comfort her. She might seem like she was okay sleeping, but it was very likely she still knew things were different around her.

The moment Demyan's palms lay flat to his daughter's stomach and chest, pain saturated him from the inside out. Her skin felt brand new against his. Warm and soft. Vera didn't stir. Demyan felt her chest rise rhythmically and her tiny heartbeat. Black eyelashes fluttered for a brief second, but she didn't open her eyes.

His baby.

His beautiful, sweet baby.

Demyan's knees hit the floor again. He was eye-level with the infant in the incubator. Resting his forehead against the hard plastic, he watched his daughter.

He cried for all that she wouldn't have.

So hard.

• • •

Documents were passed over with more care than Demyan had ever seen paper be handled by. Ivan scribbled his name across several of the sheets before giving them back to the waiting nurse.

"You understand, Mr. Lavrov, that once the ventilator tube is removed and the—"

"I understand," Ivan interrupted coolly.

Detached, Demyan felt his body float away again.

"For legal reasons, we have to explain it one last time."

Ivan sighed shakily. Eva cried.

Demyan blinked, breathed, and clenched his fists at his sides, but he didn't feel alive.

Odd how that worked. The woman he loved was brain dead only feet away, but she looked like she might feel more alive than he did.

Demyan had the hardest time to look at Gia's prone form in the hospital bed, blankets tucked in tight around her thin frame. There was no blood staining her skin and the bandages wrapping the bullet wound she sustained to her left temple were hidden by her long hair. He knew some of her blonde hair had been shaved when they attempted to operate, but it was a section underneath.

Silently, he listened as the doctor went through the procedures one last time. "The machines keeping her lungs and heart alive will be stopped. When the monitor shows a flat line for a designated period, the time will be called for death and the leads monitoring her rhythms will officially be silenced and turned off."

The room was too quiet.

In a short time, what life was left in Gia would be gone.

It already was, Demyan knew. There was no coming back from being brain dead. The life of an invalid, where she wouldn't even be able to open her eyes, was not something Gia would ever want. Demyan didn't want it for her, and neither did her parents.

It was heartbreaking and unfair, but it was best for her.

Demyan kept reminding himself of that. It didn't help much.

Somehow, Demyan found himself staring at Gia while the nurse and doctor did one last check. The tube in her throat was removed and the leads monitoring her breathing turned off. Ivan and Eva stood on either side of the bed together, each holding one of Gia's hands. Demyan couldn't move, not even when Ivan asked him over. He was stuck. Invisible cement weighed him down.

Minutes passed, but not a lot. Demyan wasn't sure how long it would take and the silence was so thick he couldn't even force himself to ask. The tightness in his chest increased as he stared at the place where Gia's wouldn't rise. Maybe he thought something amazing would happen.

This life didn't offer miracles.

Not for him.

When the monitor beeped, a flat red line crossing the screen, a crack made fissures across Demyan's heart, shattering his soul. Every head in the room turned to look at him. His heartbreak hadn't been silent. He wished to God it would have been, but it wasn't. One, aching sorrow-filled cry escaped the confines of his mind.

"I'm so sorry," Demyan whispered.

It wasn't meant for the people still breathing.

• • •

Demyan sat on the edge of his double bed in his old room at his parents' home. The darkness of the night saturated the space but for the light from the moon high in the sky reflecting through the window. Through the baby monitor, he listened to Vera's gentle puffs of air making a soothing whooshing sound with every exhale.

Three weeks after her birth, she was cleared to go home. She passed the most important tests. Her hearing and vision seemed fine. Oxygen wasn't needed as the level in her blood was perfect and she breathed without issue on her own. Her motor skills were on par with a newborn born a month and a half early, and if anything, she was at the same pace of a baby who wasn't premature. Vera took to a bottle without trouble and didn't seem to have any digestive problems.

They'd only been home three days.

Well, not really home as it was his parents', but close enough. Demyan refused to go back to the apartment where Gia was killed. Hired movers were already contracted to remove the belongings from the place and move them to a home Demyan purchased a week earlier.

For now, he and Vera would stay where they were.

A knock on the opened bedroom door drew Demyan's attention to where his father stood, somber and silent. "Yeah?"

"How're you doing?"

"Fine," Demyan said.

"Fine is a relatively useless term, Demyan. It's not a real answer, especially in this situation."

Okay, then.

"I feel like I don't know how to breathe anymore. I keep wondering what the barrel of my gun tastes like. Which would be quicker, the bullet to my temple or one in my mouth?"

Anton frowned. "Are these thoughts I need to be concerned about or are they actions you wished you could take?"

Demyan waved at the blinking baby monitor whispering

sounds. "Life won't let me go."

"Ivan wanted to know when would be a good time for Gia's sisters to come and visit Vera."

A flippant shrug fell from Demyan's shoulders. He wasn't sure what Gia's family wanted from him, frankly. They could come and go as they pleased. His daughter was just as much their blood as his, but they kept assuming his permission was needed for their presence.

"Whenever they want."

"I'm going to have to go before your mother does, you know," Anton said offhandedly.

Demyan's head jerked up, his confusion muddling up his thoughts. "What?"

"When we're older and it's time for one of us to go to wherever in the hell souls go when a person dies, I have to be the one to go first. I decided that a long time ago and whatever God is watching over us better make damn sure he takes me first. I won't live on this earth without Viviana at my side. I don't care if it's tomorrow or in twenty more years. I know she'll hurt with me gone, but she's so much better than me—stronger. She could handle it. I *need* to go first."

Demyan wasn't sure what to say to that. His father didn't give him the time to figure something out.

"But, I'm a selfish fuck like that and I always have been where your mother is concerned. I wouldn't think about who it might hurt or the people left behind. I would just … go right after her like I was meant to. So, when you say you wonder what the barrel of your gun might taste like, you can trust that I know why you feel that way. I can't empathize, but I understand. I love you and you're my son; I would never want to put you in the ground, but I'm sorry Gia went first before you. Because I know, Demyan. I *do*."

"She was mine," Demyan whispered. "My one."

"I know. It's early, though, and you're so raw, son. You're young and—"

"Don't. Christ, don't even say what you're about to say. Be honest. It's not going to get better."

"Not right now," Anton replied at the same quiet level. "It takes time. I suppose you have to learn to live without her, too. Or find a way to that works for you. I know it's not the same as what you're going through, but shortly after you were born, I was grieving, too. For my father. The best relief for me was when I held you."

"I'm not you."

Anton nodded. "I know, and I certainly don't expect you to be, either. But, your daughter needs you, Demyan. All of you, not just certain parts."

The hardest thing for Demyan was when he held Vera. Staring down at her miniature features that matched her dead mother's was suffocating. He did what he needed to for his daughter. He fed her, cared for her, and watched over her, but he was distant all the same. Depression was mentioned on more than one occasion.

Demyan brushed their comments off.

How the fuck could they possibly understand what was happening to him?

"And you need—"

Whatever his father was going to say was cut off by a high pitch wail echoing through the baby monitor. Demyan was on his feet in a second, moving past his father in the doorway, and opening the door directly across the hall. Vera quieted the moment she was in her father's arms. He didn't talk a lot to her because he didn't know what to say. Many of the motions he went through to care for her felt robotic and learned from need and force of habit.

She needed more, he knew. Unconditional love. Doting attention. His entire focus and being. Demyan wasn't sure how to give her those things being as damaged as he was.

For that, he was sorry.

Chapter Twelve

Ana

"Let's end this off with you asking me a question for a change," Sierra said.

Wariness settled in Ana. "What do you mean?"

Sierra was a demand of Ana's mother that wasn't up for discussion. Ana felt like she was doing fine, but sometimes the anxiety and anger jumped into her days without warning. Viviana suggested a therapist. Ana agreed to go. She had been having the twice weekly sessions for a month.

One of the first things she learned from Sierra was that Ana had been made a victim, but she had the choice to become a survivor.

"Well, it's always me asking a question, you talking, me prompting again, and you talking more," Sierra explained, shrugging. "I'm not saying there's anything wrong with that. You're talking, which is awesome. It shows you're healing, moving forward. I want to end today off with you asking me something about you. Anything that relates to your immediate person and emotions. Whatever. Give me something."

Ana blinked, dazed. Therapy was easy, as surprising as that was. Sierra's simple request felt anything but. Sure, there were a lot of things she could ask the woman, but only one thing came to mind: Koldan.

"I like someone," Ana said.

"This is news. You haven't mentioned someone before."

"Yeah. I liked him before the attack, too. A lot. He's been with me every step of the way."

"Has he hurt you or does he make you feel unsafe?"

"Never," Ana murmured. "He makes me feel a lot of things, but never that. He took me out for dinner last week."

"Oh?"

"It was nice and he didn't treat me like I was made of spun glass. Everyone keeps acting like I'm a china doll ready to fall off the shelf and shatter. He doesn't."

"What was your question regarding him, Ana?" Sierra asked.

Heat pinked Ana's cheeks. She forced herself to speak. "How long is normal for a woman to wait after her attack before she becomes sexually involved with someone?"

Sierra's brow lifted. "You're reacting physically to him."

It wasn't a question.

"Sure. He's handsome, intelligent, kind of sarcastic when he's in a mood, and he looks at me like I'm the most important thing to him at that moment in time. It's disconcerting."

Sierra laughed lightly. "Disconcerted isn't how you really feel about it, huh?"

"No, I like it."

"Ana, every rape survivor handles their attack and how they move forward from it in different ways. The length of time for one woman's healing and ability to open up to a man in that way isn't going to be the same as the next woman. There's so many variables. Trust. Emotions. Partnership. Physical and emotional reactions to people and events. There has to come a time when you're able to realize not every situation is going to end the way the attack did and recognizing not all men are your rapist."

"Oh," Ana said, feeling confused all over again.

"If you're expecting me to tell you it's okay for you to have a physical relationship with someone, I can't do that, Ana. Only you know if you're ready. I merely have your clues to go on."

Was she? God, she wanted to be.

"Same time next week?" Sierra asked.

Ana nodded. "Absolutely."

The drive to Ana's parents' home went quicker than she intended. Her apartment was closer to the university, but she stayed in Oceana to help Demyan with Vera. The house he bought still remained unlived in. Her brother didn't ask her for the help, but Ana wanted to.

Ana dropped her keys into the glass bowl as she shrugged off her tweed coat. "Ma, you home?"

Her mother didn't answer her call, but the man with her father walking around the corner leading to the kitchen stopped her heart in her chest. Koldan.

Ana still didn't have the first clue why he had such a strange effect on her.

Koldan held out his hand for Anton to take. Her father did, offering a smile and nod in response. Then, Koldan was walking toward Ana as her father disappeared back into the kitchen.

"Hey," he said.

"Hey. What are you doing here?"

"Having a chat."

Ana cocked a brow, curious. "Oh?"

"Yeah. Gotta get my ducks in a row, you know. No need to piss off a boss, even if he isn't my boss."

She didn't know what he was talking about.

"Anyway," Koldan said, reaching into the closet to pull his coat out. "I have to head out."

"Are you coming back anytime soon?" Ana asked.

"Do you want me to?"

Ana felt no uncertainty. "You know I do."

• • •

Grateful couldn't adequately explain how Ana felt about her father installing the heated glass structure around their in-ground pool. He kept it open for the first two years before he hired constructors to come in, design, and put up the building. It kept the bugs out in the summer and the heat in during the winter. The water maintained a warm temperature, as did the indoor space.

She wasn't practicing, but she did need a good swim to

relieve some of her stress. The session with her therapist yesterday and the question left hanging at the end was still nagging at her.

Ana dived into the water from the starting board, cutting across the surface and letting her thoughts drift away. What should have been one lap across the pool turned into four, then seven, and finally she stopped at eight. Her breaths came out in huffs as she rested along the edge of the pool. A burn settled in her worked muscles.

It didn't take her long to realize she wasn't alone in the pool house. A cool draft wafted across the water's surface as if the door to the outside had been opened.

Ana turned in the water to find Koldan sitting in one of the many lounger chairs on the tiled floor. She didn't even blink at his presence.

"Nobody was home," he said before Ana could ask a thing. "I noticed the lights on for the pool house and came to check who was back here."

"I think they took Vera to Gia's parents for a visit."

"You didn't want to go?"

"Late study group," Ana replied. "I'm surprised Demyan went. He doesn't go anywhere, now."

"Demyan's working," Koldan said. "Just left him a while ago."

Ana's confusion jumped up a notch. "Demyan doesn't have a job. He goes to school, but he doesn't work."

Well, he used to go to school. Ana didn't have a clue what her brother was doing in that regard what with Vera and everything. He didn't like to talk much. Ana didn't push him to. They spent so many years growing up at one another's throats. She didn't want to do that anymore with her brother.

She loved Demyan. The best way for her to show him that was to be there for him in whatever way she could be. Helping him to take care of Vera. Leaving him alone when everyone else kept pushing him for more. Sitting quietly in a room with him so he didn't have to feel alone.

"Actually, he does work," Koldan said. "Doing the same

thing as me."

Oh.

"Never mind, then," Ana muttered, pushing away from the wall. She drifted out into the water, free floating on her back. "Who were you looking for, my dad?"

"Nope. You."

Ana's feet touched down to the bottom of the pool as she righted herself. "Me?"

"Yeah, you. Thought we should talk. Maybe about us."

"Us."

Koldan laughed. "Don't turn into a parrot on me, Ana."

She stuck out her tongue playfully. "I didn't know there was an *us*."

"That's kind of the point. I've been trying to figure out if you wanted there to be one. Plus, I wasn't completely clear about why I was here yesterday when you came home. Whenever you ask me things, I never lie."

That was true. It was one of the things Ana liked most about Koldan. He was honest and upfront, even if it came off harsh or brash. Nonetheless, when he handed things over at face value, she didn't have to wonder about him.

"You lied yesterday?" Ana asked.

"No, I just didn't tell you what I was talking to your father about."

Ana waved his concern off. "That's not important to me. I don't have to know my father's business, Koldan."

"You do when it's about you," he replied gently. "Things might seem simple to you when it comes to who you want to see or date, but it isn't. Your father, whether you like it or not, is important. A lot like my father, I guess. Different, but kind of the same."

"You're not making any sense."

Koldan dragged a hand over his face, sighing. "I know. I'm staying in New York for a while. My father wants me hands-on doing business with Anton's guys for a while."

"What does that have to do with me?" Ana asked.

"Because while I'm here, and even when I'm not, I'd like

to be spending my time with you. You're an adult, so you can make your own decisions, but I can't, Ana. I was raised knowing respect should be the first thing I offer to those deserving of it. Pissing off your father isn't high on my list of priorities, so I needed to make sure he was okay with the fact there might be something happening between you and me."

"An us, you mean."

Koldan grinned. "Exactly."

Huh.

"And he was okay with that?" Ana questioned, skimming her hands over the water's surface.

"Yeah. Wished me luck with his little hellcat, actually."

Ana laughed loud and hard for the first time in far too long. When she finished, Koldan was standing at the edge of the pool.

"Thank you," Ana murmured.

"For what?"

"Not pitying me or treating me like I was fragile after what happened."

Koldan's brow crinkled. "Why would I do that, Ana?"

"I don't know. You just didn't. I needed that."

"What he did to you doesn't make me feel any different than how I did the first night I met you. Hair wet from swimming, smelling like chlorine, and you had the most striking eyes. I wanted to know you. I still do."

"I feel guilty," Ana said, swallowing back her rising emotions.

"Why's that?"

"Because everyone around me is heartbroken and grieving. Don't get me wrong, I am, too. At the same time, here I am thinking you might be so easy to love. You're exactly the kind of man I grew up thinking I didn't want. All you have to do is say the right words and I'll be falling head over heels. Everyone is in pain, so should I let myself be happy? It doesn't seem fair."

"Your happiness isn't dependent on how the people around you feel. Determined at times, perhaps, but not dependent. You're allowed to move forward when you're ready to, Ana. In whatever way you want and need to."

So her therapist kept telling her.

"I know."

"What are the words you need me to say?" Koldan kneeled down at the edge of the pool and rested his arms on his jean-clad knees. "Tell me the words."

"That maybe you want me, too," Ana whispered. "Even if I can be a bitch and you're way too intense. Even if I don't like the things you do and I spend six hours a day in a pool because it's the only thing I'm good at. Even if we won't work, because you know, maybe we will."

"Firstly, I have the feeling you're good for more than your skills in the water," Koldan said with a sexy smirk that sent Ana's desire spinning. "Secondly, don't think there's any maybes about it, *krasivyy*. I don't want to go anywhere and I'm pretty sure I can handle you. There's not a single thing about you I don't want to learn, Ana. Everything—I want to know it all."

Yeah, all he had to do was say the right words.

Without thinking too hard about her next actions, Ana reached out and fisted Koldan's leather jacket. She pulled him down low enough that he had to use his hands to keep steady so he wouldn't fall into the pool. His lips touched to hers hesitantly at first. When Ana didn't let up or release him from her hold, Koldan kissed her harder. His grip on the edge of the pool let go, sending him dropping into the water with Ana.

Koldan didn't seem to mind he was soaking wet because he kept kissing Ana until he'd taken the elastic out of her ponytail and weaved his fingers through her hair. A wicked heat spread from her middle outwards, smothering her in want.

Ana felt no fear or anxiety as he stared at her, waiting. The usual tendrils of caution she felt when she was close or alone with a man didn't curl around her senses to debilitate her. She was okay. With Koldan, she was far more than okay.

"You won't hurt me," Ana said, voicing her thoughts.

"Of course not. I won't pressure you into anything you're not prepared to do, either, but I need to know you're ready for this," Koldan said, wiping water from his face. "Not something physical, but *this*. Us. Because you were right. I'm intense and I don't do things half-assed, Ana. If you start moving forward with me, I'm going to take us all the way or none of it. Wherever I go, I want you to come with me. I'll probably need to make damn sure every guy within a fifty foot radius of you knows you're mine. You will always be safe with me—"

"I know I am."

"—and I want you to feel like you're the most important thing to me because I want you to be," he finished quietly.

Ana laughed, but the sound came out shaky. "You already do."

"Good." Koldan swore under his breath, chuckling. He yanked his sodden coat off and tossed it to the side of the pool. The white T-shirt he wore did nothing to hide the hard ridges of his muscular form beneath the wet fabric. Ana's mouth went dry. "That's a two-thousand dollar jacket and it's ruined."

She continued gawking at his body. "You didn't have to get in the pool."

"I think I did. You're staring, Ana."

"Yep."

Because he was fucking *gorgeous* and every part of her knew it.

"Cross-country running and rugby," Koldan said, smiling slyly. "It's kept me in good shape."

"Yep," Ana repeated. "Don't worry about sending me running, Koldan."

Koldan moved in closer until they were pressed tightly together. His hands twisted into the sides of her two-piece bathing suit while he skimmed his nose along her cheekbone. "You okay?"

"So okay," she promised.

His hand skipped under her top, his palm resting flat on her lower back. "Tell me if you need to stop."

"I will, but right now, please don't."

Koldan took his time to lavish attention on Ana with his hands and mouth. The softest touches of his fingers along her bare skin were aided by the caresses of his lips across her jaw and neck. Ana didn't rush him to go faster. The slow building of his intent created a spiral of desire twisting inside like silk ribbons.

Water was the most soothing, safe place Ana had ever known, but when Koldan asked her to get out of the pool with him she didn't refuse. They found themselves in Ana's old room, still exploring with their hands and lips as wet clothes were shed to the floor. He was beautiful with clothes on, but glorious with them off. His fingers interweaved with hers as he dropped to his knees. Ana couldn't concentrate on anything but staring at Koldan while he watched her down between her thighs.

His tongue at her slit was heaven. He tunneled in slow at first, his nose nudging along her clit with just enough pressure to send shivers racing down her spine. The tempo of his strokes sped up, his tongue lapping from between her folds to her throbbing nub before she had blinked. Ana's quiet moan turned into a sharp gasp when Koldan encased her with his lips and sucked, throwing her off into a precipice of blinding bliss.

A tender kiss landed down on her inner thigh. "It should never hurt, Ana. This, what we do, will never hurt you. I couldn't hurt you."

Ana nodded; she knew that and he didn't have to tell her.

"I'm not going to treat you like you're some breakable doll any other time, but right now, it's not the same. We can slow down or stop. You're making the calls here," Koldan said, standing and keeping their hands locked together. His cock rested between their bodies, but Ana didn't feel the slightest bit of fear at the sensation of its pulse matching his heartbeat. "Whatever you want."

The zinging hum from her orgasm was dissipating. Ana wanted it back. With Koldan, of course she did. "I don't want to stop. I want you."

When he asked for one, she found him a condom from a package her mother made sure was always available in the dresser, no questions asked. Instead of finding herself with her back to the bed, Koldan had her straddle him. She took him slowly, the slickness from her sex easing the first, full thrust of his shaft. No pain intruded on her moment, just a sweet, burning heat as his cock stretched her full of him.

All the while, her one hand tangled in his short hair at the nape of his neck and her other scored lines down his back. Ana's eyes fluttered closed as his lips ghosted along the seam of her mouth and his hands drove up her back.

Because it did feel good. So fucking *good*.

Ana shuddered, delicious sparks of pleasure charring her nerves. It was new and that was scary. Her body seemed to know what it wanted and she did what felt right—natural. Koldan allowed her to set the pace and followed her lead. A leisurely rhythm. There was no frenzy to her movements, no rush in her want. The passion still climbed and the fever still raced. It didn't have to be furious and quick between them to give her what she needed.

The sensation of Koldan's cock filling her over and over as Ana rode him felt like a drug being fed straight to her veins. His heady groans fell muffled to her cheek. When she came again, she stilled in her bliss, crying out. The final remainders of the walls she'd built shattered. He followed right behind, his shaking hands holding her snug in his lap. The power behind gaining her control and life back again sent a fresh round of emotions rising and tears falling.

"*Shhh*, I got you," she heard Koldan breath. "It's okay, *krasivyy*."

It was, now.

And it would only get better.

Epilogue

Demyan

"You want me to come with you?" Ana asked. "Koldan can watch Vera."

"No," Demyan said, a pressure bearing down on his throat. "I want to be alone for a while. Just me."

Ana seemed to understand. "Okay. Come to Auntie, Vera."

Demyan handed over his squirming child, her calls for him rising louder as he walked up the pathway past the gravestones. Nearly six months to the day had passed since they put the love of his life in the ground here. The doctors took Gia off life support on the fourth of December, only three days after Vera was born. Then, they buried Gia just five days later. The ground hadn't been frozen enough for the burial to be held off until spring.

Too many breaths from his lungs.

Too many beats from his heart.

Demyan missed her funeral because he couldn't stand to go. He couldn't watch the casket go down. Ivan called him a selfish bastard for the choice, but Gia's father didn't understand. Demyan didn't know how to explain that dirt should never have covered her first. Instead, he stayed at the hospital with Vera and rocked her until his arms were numb and the tears had stopped coming. Demyan hadn't let another tear fall after that day.

No matter how many times someone offered, Demyan refused to come to the graveyard. This was the first time and he wasn't entirely sure why he had even come today. The two calla lilies in his hand shook from the tremors rocking his fist clenched around the thick stems.

The first six months of his daughter's life was spent in a

haze of grief and the black bleakness that came along with anguish and agony. He barely remembered learning how to feed and burp her, or even change her diaper. The sleepless nights weren't really sleepless when Demyan couldn't sleep at all.

Life was waiting for him to move again. The world hadn't stopped turning just because his ended. It might have been better if it had.

Demyan stopped at a sleek, black marble headstone. Her name was crisp, clear and bold across the middle. The dates were haunting to him. The sound of his daughter's babyish giggles traveled up to his spot. The coldness started seeping in his veins again.

Gia was so much more than this place. More than a marker and a grave.

She was his first kiss. His best friend, even when she couldn't stand him. She'd been the first person he met coming off the stage at his high school graduation and she was the same six-year-old girl who held his hand when he walked into kindergarten. Her initials were carved into the bedpost of the bed in his old room, on the trunk of the tree in his parents' backyard, and anywhere he'd ever traveled, he left a piece of her behind. That way, if he ever had to go back alone, he could always find where he left her memory.

He had fifty-six movie stubs, one for each one they went to when they were teens, in a shoebox in his closet. All the concert tickets they saw together were in the box, too. The black hair elastic she wrapped around the bedroom doorknob in his old room at his parents' so she wouldn't forget it was still there. Her ballet flats were still in his car.

"Papa gone," Demyan said, rolling to his back in the sand.

Gia skipped around his body, kicking up the wet sand on the beach in Little Odessa. Demyan could see Ma talking to Gia's Papa. Ma was crying.

"Gone how?" Gia asked.

"I don't know. Gone. Ma said."

She fell down beside him, a tiny, sandy hand finding his. "I'm here."

Demyan smiled. Gia was never gone.

She was his life. He only ever knew her.

All of his days were marked with her fingerprints. She left nothing on him untouched.

"You coming, Demyan?" Gia asked. The bottom of her yellow summer dress was muddied from their exploration in the woods. She kept trying to wipe it away, huffing in that way of hers, but the dirt was still there. "Well, are you?"

"Yeah, I'm coming."

She was seven. He was six.

"You going to follow me?"

"I'm always gonna follow you, Gia."

"Good, 'cause you don't know the trail."

Demyan blinked out of the memory, feeling a heaviness rest on his chest.

Another one slammed into him just as fast.

"How much do you love me?" Gia asked.

"What do you mean love?"

The sounds of her tenth birthday party echoed in the background, but they never did play well with others, so they had hidden themselves under a table. Someone called for Gia, but the two didn't move from their hiding spot.

Gia drew a purple heart on the floor. She was probably going to get in trouble for that. "You know, like love."

"Ma tells me she loves me," Demyan said, turning his palm over so Gia could doodle on his hand.

"No, not like that."

"Papa tells Ma he loves her. Like crazy, he says. Like nobody knows."

Gia grinned. "Yeah, like that. Do you love me like that, Demyan?"

"I love you like I love you, Gia."

Everything. Every. Single. Moment.

All of it had been spent with her.

"I'm sorry," Demyan whispered. "I should have waited for you. You should have been my first, too. I thought you didn't want to be like that with me, Gia."

"We've always been like that, Demyan." She wiped the wet lines

from her cheeks. "Do you love her like you love me?"

"Nobody loves you like I love you. I don't love anyone like I love you."

He tried to pull up memories of his childhood that didn't include Gia in one way or another. Not one came to mind. His younger years were spent chasing behind her. Most of his teenage years were spent learning how to love her in an entirely new way.

Life was a killer. It had taken everything from him. He gave it all to her and it was gone.

Demyan pulled open the front door and once more, handed his heart over. "Gia."

She was beautiful even when she cried.

"I can't do it. I can't marry him, Demyan. He's not you."

Demyan pressed the heel of his palms to his eyes to rid the burning sensation behind his lids. The air coming from his lungs felt hot and thick as it rushed out in painful pants.

"How am I supposed to do this without you?" Demyan asked, staring up at the sky. He didn't want to think of Gia in the ground, so he refused to look there. "I don't know how to be me without you, Gia. Because there's nothing left here. Nothing inside me. I keep looking, but I can't find it. I'm empty. I needed to learn how to hide the way I felt, but I can't remember how to feel anything, now. It's gone. I am so cold without you."

Demyan turned to look back at his six-month-old daughter in her aunt's arms. She was waving to Koldan and smiling brightly in her cheerful, innocent way. The only thing his baby needed to be happy was love.

He wasn't sure he knew how to give that anymore.

Vera was his child, the one thing he had left of Gia, and he didn't know how to love her.

"She is so beautiful," Demyan whispered. "She's got my black hair, but your curls. The shape of my eyes, but blue like yours. Every time I look at her, I see you staring back at me. I don't know how to do this. I don't know how to live when what made me feel alive isn't here.

"People break, you know. It's what we were always told. Their hearts break. Apparently, I'm not like everybody else, Gia, because I fucking shattered. There are shards of me everywhere. There's nothing that can put me back together." Demyan kneeled down, placing the two calla lilies on top of green grass. "One for me and one for her. I can't come back here again. I just won't. But, I wanted you to know I loved you. God, how I loved *you*, Gia."

As fast as Demyan made his way up the path to Gia's grave, he left it. The harshness of his deadened emotions froze his veins with every step he took.

"Papa! Papa!"

Vera babbled louder the closer Demyan came to where his daughter, his sister, her boyfriend still stood waiting.

"Demyan?" Ana asked.

"Can you watch her for the rest of the day?" Demyan asked.

Ana shifted Vera on her hip. "Sure, if you want."

"Good. Thanks. I'll move her car seat over into Koldan's truck."

"Demyan, Gia would—"

"Don't, Ana," Demyan said. "Don't ever mention her name to me again. Just *don't*."

With that, he turned to the direction where he parked his vehicle earlier. He didn't miss the sad question trailing behind him.

"Why doesn't he cry?" Ana asked.

"Broken men don't know how to," Koldan replied quietly.

Demyan had to agree. Every bit of pain came from his own hands. He allowed a man to be invited into the safe haven that was his family's home. Ana's attack followed. The way he handled that issue led to Gia's murder. Lives around him were irrevocably changed because of his choices. It was the worst and truest form of devastation. That's who he was.

The least Demyan could do was save his daughter from being hurt by him, too. He didn't want to wake up one day and realize that he resented his innocent child for keeping him from following her mother like he always promised to.

There was one other thing that stayed nailed to the back of Demyan's mind, too. Liam Dolan. The man promised to take two of the things Demyan loved. He only took one.

All Demyan ever did was ruin beautiful things.

Vera wouldn't be one of them.

ABOUT THE AUTHOR

Bethany-Kris is a Canadian author, lover of much, and mother to three very young sons, one cat, and two dogs. A small town in Eastern Canada where she was born and raised is where she has always called home. With her boys under her feet, a snuggling cat, barking dogs, and a spouse calling over his shoulder, she is nearly always writing something ... when she can find the time.

Find Bethany-Kris at:
Her website www.bethanykris.com,
or on Facebook at www.facebook.com/bethanykriswrites,
on her blog at www.bethanykris.blogspot.ca,
or on Twitter - @BethanyKris.

Sign up to Bethany-Kris's New Release Newsletter here:
http://eepurl.com/bf9lzD

MORE BY BETHANY-KRIS

The Russian Guns
The Arrangement
The Life
The Score
Demyan & Ana
Shattered

Filthy Marcellos
Filthy Marcellos: Lucian
Filthy Marcellos: Giovanni
Filthy Marcellos: Dante

Watch for more at www.bethanykris.com

www.ingramcontent.com/pod-product-compliance
Lightning Source LLC
Chambersburg PA
CBHW061251170626
46809CB00007B/2949